PARADISE SHORES

A NOIR HORROR THRILLER

ALEXANDER SEMENYUK

This is a work of fiction. Names, characters, places, and incidents are products of the author's imagination or are used fictitiously and are not to be construed as real. Any resemblance to actual events, locations, organizations, or persons, living or dead, is entirely coincidental.

World Castle Publishing, LLC
Pensacola, Florida
Copyright © Alexander Semenyuk 2022
Hardback ISBN: 9798835670574
Paperback ISBN: 9781958336267
eBook ISBN: 9781958336274
First Edition World Castle Publishing, LLC, July 11, 2022
http://www.worldcastlepublishing.com
Licensing Notes
Cover: Boris Bashirov
Editor: Maxine Bringenberg

CHAPTER ONE

I, Ida Clifton, received a devastating letter at the age of thirty-three. Other people may have welcomed the news I got as something wonderful, but not I. It was a letter informing me that my grandmother had passed away, leaving me her entire estate. All I had to do was go and claim it on the island where she lived. Strangely, I'd never even been there because she traveled to us for all the family gatherings, not the other way around. I had planned to go there several times, but each time something came up. Sadly, in retrospect, it was never anything more important than seeing her alive one last time. It was sad news, and instead of being excited, I went forth to the island with a heavy heart. Little did I know the horrors that awaited me on the island of Paradise Shores.

The sky was tightly covered by a wrinkled grey blanket of gloomy clouds. Waves hit the side of the ship one by one, their efforts becoming more and more violent and persistent as the wind over the sea began to pick up speed. I was standing on the deck observing all around me, wrapped in my black coat, but underneath I wore only a summer dress, and my legs were cold.

My curiosity and sense of adventure kept me outside despite my discomfort. The name of the ship was "Dead Glory," not a very promising moniker, but it was the only ship that was able to take me to Paradise Shores this week. It was captained by a short, middle-aged man with a bald head and small dark eyes, Gonzalo.

The grim horizon did not yet reveal our destination, the island where my grandmother Isabella and grandfather Michael had lived out their last years. Michael died first, but strangely Grandmother staged the funeral on the mainland instead of having mourners come to Paradise Shores. Grandfather was buried in the small rural town where he was born. I still remember the young priest who did the service; he was very kind.

The fact that I was the one who received the entire inheritance upset many others in the family, but I was most surprised of all.

The clouds got darker, and it began to drizzle, so I went inside my cabin. As I reached the door, the rain came down in buckets.

The cabin was cozy, with typical wood-paneled walls. There were two small anchors hung, one painting of a ship, and several ropes tied in different knots. I had a small berth, which I sat on and looked out the porthole. The ship was rocking wildly as the waves picked up tremendously. I could feel my heart strongly beating against the walls of my chest. I felt a mixture of excitement about the storm and the adventure, plus fear of the unknown and sadness over my grandmother's passing. Perhaps I could describe my emotions as similar to the sea and the changes it was constantly going through.

I saw the crew struggling outside, yet they were managing just fine. Gonzalo did not strike me as the most trustworthy character around, but he was the only one able to take me to the island — or should I say, willing to. I had no idea why other ships had no interest in going to Paradise Island. Perhaps I should have asked around more. Nevertheless, the crew of Gonzalo and his three men were dealing with the storm for now, or at least that's how it seemed to me, but I was no expert on sailing.

Suddenly I was thrown violently from one wall to the other. I heard a loud sound and felt a powerful impact. We had hit something.

Gonzalo knocked, then entered my cabin with his small eyes round with worry. "We must go on a small boat now, Lady Ida, as the boat is stuck on a large rock. My men will stay here since the boat can carry only two. And we must go now. I'll leave you on the shore and will find help at the port. We are not far from the island, and the storm is calming down now."

Indeed he was right—the wind was slower, and the rain had stopped, but the damage was done. He assured me that the ship was in such a position that it wouldn't sink and that the three men were not in danger.

I climbed down a rope ladder into a tiny lifeboat with Gonzalo. I had to hold my backpack as it was so crammed in the boat, even just for the two of us. He started the motor, and the boat began moving through waves, farther and farther from the unfortunate "Dead Glory."

"Lady, it's okay, it's okay."

Gonzalo was looking at me, his eyes filled with worry. He clearly saw how nervous and scared I was, and I thought perhaps I had misjudged his character based on appearances.

"We'll be fine."

Gonzalo pointed forward, and I now could see the outline of the island and even some homes clinging to its cliffs. We were close indeed. The waves were manageable now, and the dark clouds were rapidly disappearing, displaying the rays of God's lamp, the sun.

"Over there, that's the port."

Gonzalo indicated a long pier, and I could see some boats and ships there but no people as we got closer.

Once at the pier, Gonzalo threw the rope around one of the wooden columns and tied it tightly. He proceeded to help me out of the boat. "First, let me quickly find a policeman to guide you, Lady Ida. This part of town isn't the best; I've heard bad things about it when I have stayed here."

He hurried along the pier and then excitedly flagged down a man standing on the deck of a boat, whom he clearly knew. Middle-aged, he had short black hair, a strong jaw, large blue eyes, and an aquiline nose. I thought he was handsome.

"Alain! So lucky to see you out here!" yelled Gonzalo.

Alain stepped off his craft and onto the pier. They embraced.

"This young woman needs to get to Clifton Estates. She has all the documents needed for her stay. A lawyer has been waiting for her there. And I need help — I have men stuck on my boat out in the sea. We wrecked. They are stuck on a rock!"

"Please, let me come too. It'll be better if you don't split up. Maybe someone is injured," I suggested.

Gonzalo was surprised but shrugged and accepted my offer. We clambered onto Alain's ship. It was a small, pretty yacht and not an inexpensive vessel. From what I could observe, Alain seemed quite well off. But the fact that he was a friend of someone like Gonzalo showed that he wasn't an arrogant rich man.

As the ship smoothly split the water and the sun shone, we could see the outline of the large rocks and the small ship aground on them.

"We have to drop anchor here and take the motorboat."

Alain dropped the anchor, and we got into a good-sized tender, much nicer than the tiny one Gonzalo had brought me in. As we got close to Gonzalo's wrecked ship, we could not see anyone on board.

Alain's face became grim. "Why aren't they on deck?"

"Probably resting in the cabin," said Gonzalo, but he was clearly nervous.

Alain deftly tossed a loop of rope onto a cleat on the boat's stern, then used another rope to tightly attach us. He proceeded to climb the ladder up to the ship first, and then he assisted me and Gonzalo.

There was a line of what looked like red paint leading toward the hatch. I looked at the men and could see by their reaction that it was indeed blood.

Alain suddenly drew a gun from underneath his coat, which greatly startled me, but it also made me feel more secure. Gonzalo opened the hatch to below and used his flashlight to peer inside. He led the way as we descended the steps.

There was a rock protruding through a hole in the corner of the hold, but the water was trickling in very slowly. The trail of blood stretched across the floor and toward the hole, but there was no one to be seen.

Gonzalo shook his head. "My God, the rumors were true...I should not have come back here."

"What rumors?" I asked.

"It's important that we leave now and talk later," said Alain.

I climbed back up first, followed by the two men. Gonzalo took a few things, including his ship's log, Alain picked up my suitcase, and we all boarded the motorboat again. Confused and worried, I sat watching their grim faces. Only the sounds of the motor and the boat dashing through the water cut the silence.

This was an unsettling way to begin my trip to claim my grandmother's estate, to say the least. Gonzalo's reference to rumors was swirling around my brain. I was creating all kinds of possibilities with my imagination.

When we safely reached the port again aboard Alain's ship, he invited us to sit with him in a large cabin. "You must be very startled right now, Ida. You heard Gonzalo mention the rumors. Here are some things I can tell you with certainty since you will be staying on our island. We have three major regions on this island. Cristium is the large town you see beyond this port. The hillside village is part of it. Burg is a large village in the forest region, and there is Everett, around the west side of the island, which has a small harbor with farmland, a fisherman's village, and a lighthouse.

"Recently, there have been people going missing when out on the water, in the fields or forests. The actual towns have been safe. The rumors are that there is some kind of a creature that stays away from populous areas but hunts people in the wild."

The story sounded ridiculous, but I was chilled. I took a deep breath and turned to look at the town. The breeze on the water picked up. Was this why Grandma had been so careful about never inviting anyone to see her? Why had she stayed here, then? Why did anyone?

"How many people have gone missing?"

Alain shook his head. "In the past two years, at least forty. We now get barely any tourism. The economy is doing well, regardless; we are very self-sufficient, and we still deliver great goods to the mainland, so the residents prosper."

"Will you guide me to my grandmother's home?"

Alain smiled, showing beautiful white teeth. He looked like a movie star. "Of course, with pleasure. And Gonzalo, you can use my motorboat to get back when you're ready. Take any supplies you need."

Gonzalo, despite Alain's kindness, looked miserable. His crew were likely dead, and his business was ruined. I felt great pity for the man.

As Alain and I stepped onto the pier, Gonzalo got into the motorboat. We waved goodbye and turned toward the town, and Alain told me more. "That poor man, Gonzalo...it's like a curse. Two years ago, his family was killed when a train went off its rails on a bridge. You might have read about it or heard it on the radio. It took him a while to get back to work, but he did eventually, and now this. I don't know how he handles it still. Maybe it's his faith."

"Which religion?"

"He's a Christian; how about you?"

"I am too, and you?"

His mouth twisted wryly. "I don't subscribe to any religion."

There was a lot of movement now in the town. People were on the sidewalks, coming and going, and opening doors of shops and wiping rainwater off outdoor tables and chairs.

"Hungry? There is a great bakery nearby."

"Yes!"

My stomach rumbled, and I felt exhausted in the aftermath of the stress and adrenaline that had been coursing through my body. Sitting down for a coffee and baked goods sounded great. We walked together up a curvy street leading into a higher part of the town. It was paved with beautiful light brown cobblestones. All around, there were flowers, bushes, and colorful homes filled with personality. The people seemed to be going about their lives calmly and cheerfully. It was almost as though we were in another world, and the earlier events had been a strange dream.

Up ahead, I saw a small building faced in red

stone. Above the door was a large plank which read "La Dame Ava Cafe and Bakery." Alain noticed me looking at it and confirmed that it was the place we were headed.

As I stepped inside the small, cozy café, the aroma of freshly baked pastries and coffee filled my lungs and had almost a therapeutic effect on my mind and body, as some of the tension seemed to ease. We sat down at one of the small tables by the window, and after looking at all the options, I chose a croissant with salmon and boiled eggs. Alain got himself a ham sandwich, and we ordered two coffees.

I was so hungry I forgot my manners and ate the croissant as quickly as I could, not even waiting for my coffee. Alain seemed to not care at all, as he did pretty much the same with his food. We were both already more relaxed when the hot drinks were poured.

"So, Alain, did you know my grandmother?"

"Isabella Clifton? Of course! Everyone knew her. She helped a lot of people in these parts."

"How so?"

"Finances. She gave money to struggling businesses, fed the poor in the area...wonderful woman."

I stirred my coffee. "She was wonderful...I wish I had spent more time with her."

"Life is very unpredictable and sudden. That's just how it goes, yes?" Alain sipped his coffee.

"I suppose so," I answered, then sighed. "I think she loved this island, and from what you say, the people here."

Alain smiled as he looked at me. "The people here are very kind and friendly, very faithful as well. These recent hardships have been testing everyone, but still, everyone finds positivity...almost everyone."

Quickly I changed the subject. "So, what do you think about her property?"

"What do you mean? It's beautiful, in a great location. Do you intend to sell it?"

I shrugged. "I'm not sure yet. I have to meet the man in charge of handling the transition and hear the official reading of the will."

"I see," he nodded. "Well, this was a good break, yes? Shall I take you to the estate now?"

I smiled and thanked him. There was a good aura about him. It made me feel safe.

CHAPTER TWO

We walked back out onto the beautiful stone-paved street, and Alain pointed up to a side road. I realized something strange just then.

"Alain, I have not seen a single car here!"

Alain's eyes twinkled. "Cars are banned on our island. Been this way since they were announced to the world. We use bikes, horses, carriages, and everyone walks, of course. It sometimes makes the loading of many products tricky when farmers and businesses bring them to the harbor."

"Oh wow. That's very unusual." I paused. "I guess I like it. So, we will walk to Grandmother's estate? How long will it take?"

"Only half an hour from here, higher up the

hill. It overlooks most of the town, and you have the ocean view as well."

We trudged along for a few minutes. "Alain, how long have you lived here?"

"My whole life. Like you, I got an inheritance, but from my parents. I would rather have them with me now than all their money. Tragically, the sea took them."

"I'm sorry to hear that, Alain."

"No, no. Life is beautiful. They are still with me, watching over me."

"I believe that also," I said, sincerely.

Alain stopped and pointed into the distance. "You see, at this angle, we can see our lighthouse."

It was the widest and tallest lighthouse I had ever seen. The spiral paint job was red on white, different from the typical black. We could actually see someone standing on the deck outside the light, and beyond it was a field with what looked like a farm.

"Do you know who that is?"

"Of course. Reficul Raul, our lighthouse tenant and a good farmer as well. He is a very beloved figure all over the island."

"How old is he?"

"Actually, he's quite young, only thirty-five, but he manages like a veteran."

I noticed an enormous tree in the field near the lighthouse, one tall trunk branching off into four sections. It looked like a birch, but at this distance, I could not be sure.

"Well, come along, Ida. We will be there soon."

I continued on the stony path with Alain.

There was a pretty little flower shop on our left with a vibrant garden right behind it. There were kids playing in a small field, kicking a ball to each other. Their families were laughing and talking. Everyone seemed friendly. It amazed me knowing that there was such trouble with an unknown killer in these parts. This positivity surely was also why my grandma had loved it here.

We turned the bend, and just up another hill was a large gate with metal letters arching over it, reading, "Clifton."

"Well, we are here," Alain announced.

"Wow." I exhaled slowly as I gazed at my grandmother's home. Behind the gate was a large lawn with a flower garden and a fountain in the center of it. A mansion stood beyond it. I was amazed. "It's huge!"

Alain laughed. "Yes, it's the largest house on the island, Ida."

Alain opened the gate, and I followed him onto a gravel path along the left side of the lawn.

The air was sweet with the scent of the flower garden as we got closer to the house. At the door stood a tall thin man who must have seen us coming. His green shirt created a Christmas-like look against the red front door of the mansion.

I stopped for a moment and gazed up, absorbing the details of this gorgeous and mighty house. Ivory columns and large windows with blue frames graced the front, with a flower box or a bird feeder at almost every one. Someone was maintaining this home well.

"Hello," said a man approaching us. "I'm Solario, the lawyer entrusted with handling this estate. I hope you are Ida Clifton?"

"Yes, indeed I am."

Solario shook my hand. "I'd love to make this quick for you. I have all the documents inside. Once we sign all of them, I'll be gone, and Nigel Rufus, Mrs. Clifton's butler, will give you the tour of everything you'll officially own."

I nodded.

"Ida, I will be on my way now," said Alain.

I turned and thanked him sincerely. He assured me that if I needed anything, he'd be glad to help and left.

"Please, Ida, follow me." Solario held the door for me. He seemed tense, even irritated, but he looked like he was trying to do his best to be polite.

I entered the house, and my mouth dropped in awe. The interior was stunning, to say the least. A large crystal chandelier hung down from a tall painted ceiling. It was like a work of art in a large chapel. The floors were made from white marble. Solario showed me into a room on the right. It was vast, with two large white couches and a glass coffee table. I sat on a white couch as he placed the papers on the table and pulled up a chair.

"Everything in this home, in the bank, the grounds. All of it will officially belong to you once you sign these."

I took the time to carefully read through the documents. When I saw the amount of money in the local bank, my eyes almost popped out. All the paperwork seemed in order. I was indeed about to become extraordinarily wealthy, but my heart was still heavy about my grandmother's death.

Then as I read the will, I noticed a clause. *Only if the inheritor lives on the island for ten years.* I looked up at Solario, confused. "What does this mean? I cannot sell the estate?"

"Ah...yes, Ida. It means you inherit this house only after you live on the island for at least ten years. However, you can have the money in the bank and leave if that's what you choose to do."

"What would happen then? With the estate, I mean."

"It would be given to the people here. As it states further."

This seemed odd, but I felt that I could at least try. I hesitated only a moment. "Well, I will sign. I guess time will tell."

With a trembling hand, I became the new owner of Clifton Estates on Paradise Shores. Solario made copies of the documents for himself and left me the originals after notarizing everything. He told me that the butler, Nigel, lived in a small house to the left of the mansion.

A strange and overwhelming feeling of anxiety overcame me as he left the building. It all seemed so unofficial, not regular. Just like that? And now what? I was to be in charge of it all? I sat in place, thinking. I probably ought to go out and meet the butler Nigel, but I first needed to calm down.

I looked up. Also, in this room, the ceiling was high, and there was a gold-painted chandelier with winking crystals.

"Ohhh...."

I slowly got up and walked back into the main foyer. I stared up the wide, curving staircase leading to the second floor, and further up the wall, there were two portraits of my grandmother and grandfather.

I mounted the steps. The stairs in my old home always squeaked, so with each step up, I expected this, but these were perfection, utterly and completely silent. It struck me as a lack of personality.

I approached the paintings. Both were of them in their sixties, the likenesses very well executed. I had the uncomfortable feeling they were both watching me. I glanced to the right and was about to go into the closest room, but hesitated and went back down. It was time to get the butler.

I went out through the front door and took a path along the left side of the mansion, surrounded by beautifully tended flowers and plants, their scent bringing joy to my senses. Suddenly I noticed an older lady with grey hair kneeling by some flowers, trimming leaves. She heard my steps and, with a big smile, got to her feet as quickly as her body allowed it. She was very slim, with a wrinkled face and a kind smile.

She approached me and took my hands. "Oh my goodness! You must be sweet Miss Ida, finally… is it you?"

I smiled. "Yes indeed, nice to meet you, Miss…?"

"Oh, my manners, the excitement got to me. I'm Nella, and I have been taking care of gardens since long before even your grandparents moved here."

"Very nice to meet you, Nella. I am actually looking for Nigel."

"Oh yes, keep heading that way toward the servants' house. I saw him earlier. I'll continue working. See you later, dear."

"Thank you, Nella."

Now I could understand the energy radiating

from the beautiful gardens. This kind woman had made me feel welcome and cared for.

As I reached the servants' house, I was amazed, and at the same time pleased, to see how pretty and large it was. Its walls were built from black and grey stones, and the roof was made of red tiles. The door was black-painted wood. I saw a bell hanging at the side of the door and pulled a rope to ring it. Almost immediately, an older man with a round face and a serious but gentle look appeared.

"Miss Ida?"

"Indeed, and you are Nigel?"

He inclined his head. "Yes. It's my pleasure to welcome our new queen of the house. Please, allow me to give you a full tour of everything."

"Of course, Nigel, thank you so much."

Nigel regarded me for a moment. "I feel the same humbleness and kindness emanating from you as it did from your wonderful grandmother, our dear Isabella."

I was a bit surprised by this frankness. "I'm glad you feel that way already. I am also glad to be here." I felt encouraged, thanks to these new pleasant encounters.

Nigel closed the door behind him and beckoned me to follow him. I mentioned that I had already met Nella as he told me some things about the gardens.

"Your grandmother loved these gardens," Nigel said, his eyes a bit misty. He led me to a spot behind the house with a small white metal table and a beautiful wooden chair. The little patch of gravel on which they sat was surrounded by splendid flowers. "This is where our dear lady had tea every morning."

Our tour continued. Nigel pointed out five entrances to the main house. He opened one of the doors to show me into the vast kitchen.

"Daniel Baker is the name of our chef. He is assisted by two ladies, Silvia and Michelle. And there is also Mark, a very regular fellow, who does his job well."

Nigel explained that the meadows were taken care of by a few farmers who were automatically paid weekly by the bank. He then began the tour of the mansion itself.

As we stood in the entry, Nigel explained that the estate had belonged to a family called Blackswan prior to my grandparents' acquiring it. At that point, it had stood abandoned for years, and no one really knew what had happened to the last of the Blackswans. "Perhaps, if you are interested, you can find out more at our library," he finished.

The mansion had a large basement. It wasn't decorated like the rest of the house. There was a simple concrete floor, lots of storage shelves, and freezers for the food and other household supplies. A small old couch sat in front of a fireplace. Nigel said that often the servants rested there to take a short break in front of the fire.

We went back up the stairs and into the dining room. Yet another massive and glorious chandelier hung above a long mahogany table with chairs of the same color around it.

We went up the curving staircase to the bedrooms. The main guest room had a fireplace with a brass fender and two green loveseats next to it.

"Do you want to take your grandmother's room?" Nigel asked as we entered it.

It was lovely, with silk draperies and bed curtains, but I shook my head. I chose an unused room. It had a large soft bed with pale green bedding, and the walls were painted light blue. On the walls were various paintings of ships and the ocean, and by a tall cheval mirror was the portrait of a young woman with long black hair and large black eyes. She sat in a chair by the cliffs in a black dress with the ocean waves in the background.

"This is Eleanor, the beauty of the Blackswans. This is the only painting from the other family your grandparents kept. I can remove it for you, my lady."

"No!" I went closer to it and touched it in fascination. "She was truly a beauty indeed...those eyes...it's as though I can see into her soul." I turned and looked at Nigel. "I don't understand how a painting can be so lifelike. I will keep it here."

"That's fine, as you wish."

"Do you know what happened to her?" I asked.

Nigel shrugged and lifted both hands. "No one knows, but there are rumors."

"What kind of rumors?"

Nigel fixed me with a stern look. "My lady, I think some things are best left in the past. I really don't understand these things that people speak of. Perhaps you could check at the library. They have things written about the Blackswan family there."

I knew no more information was forthcoming. "Thank you, Nigel."

Nigel excused himself to oversee the lunch preparations. I had brought up the one small bag I had with me, so I fell on top of the soft green bed, finally able to fully relax.

I actually drifted off to sleep, and in my dream, I was transported to a beautiful garden by the ocean. The flowers of all shapes and sizes were all colored in various shades of red. I looked beyond the flowers towards the shore. There I saw a young woman in a red dress—the same girl in the painting. The ocean waves started to rise higher and higher. The wind began to howl as all the flower petals began to fall and swirl around me. I was distracted for a moment but then looked back to see Eleanor again, and to my shock, there was only the red dress lying on the shore. She was gone. The dress got wet and then was pulled out to sea by the mighty waves crashing unto the shore. I tried to scream her name, but my voice was muted.

I woke up with the sound of a bell near my door and a light knocking. Then I heard Nigel's voice apologizing and letting me know that the food was ready. He asked if I wanted my meal brought to my room, but I assured him I was fine.

I humbly and happily descended the stairs and situated myself at the head chair at the dining table. It was strange because there was only one place setting — mine. A moment later, a pretty young female servant came in. She had curly black hair, thin eyebrows, a small delicate nose, large brown eyes, and a rather serious expression. She introduced herself as Michelle and bowed her head. Michelle then asked what I'd like to drink. I decided on sparkling water and weak red wine. She left and shortly reappeared with both. Following her came a male servant about her age. I straight away realized it was Mark because Nigel's word "regular" popped into my head immediately upon seeing him. I hid a small smile, wondering if I was being rude.

Mark smiled as he placed my plate in front of me. It was fresh fish, steamed broccoli, grilled peppers, and brown rice with spring onion mixed in it.

The food was delicious, perhaps the best I'd ever had in quality, but the simple dishes my parents used to make for me in my childhood when we were so poor still stood out in my mind more than any others.

After I finished, another female servant, Silvia, helped Mark clear up. Silvia was taller than the other servants, and she had chestnut hair and lots of freckles, which went well with her green eyes. She was a very pleasant woman.

How fortunate I was to be left all this.

I asked Nigel about the bank on the island and the payments of salaries for everyone and everything. Nigel assured me that, as Solario had told me, everything had been set up. He then showed me to my grandmother's room, swung a painting aside on hidden hinges, and gave me the combination for the safe hidden there. It was filled with cash. I would not have to go to the bank for a while.

Since the lunch was a late one, I decided to take a stroll to get my bearings in the neighborhood. Nigel asked if I needed someone with me, but I assured him I would be just fine.

I changed into a simpler outfit: a brown tweed skirt, white blouse, and brown jacket. I put on brown walking shoes and a neat brown hat. I was ready for my first little venture alone.

"Nights come early on the island," Nigel warned, as I went out the door. I could already see the sun starting to dip slightly, although I still had a good amount of time.

I went beyond the gate and onto the cobblestone road. Despite being a bit fatigued still, my short nap had given me some energy, so I felt in good shape to do this. I decided to walk back down into the town.

The air was fresh and neither too warm nor too cool. An occasional breeze threatened to lift my hat. Most of the people I saw on the streets passing by gave me a smile or a nod—very different from the impersonal cities on the mainland. In several of the streets, I saw some people setting up candles and oil lamps for nighttime, cooking food outside, and tuning up guitars. I went all the way past the café Alain had taken me, La Dame Ava. I pondered whether or not to go down to the harbor, but I saw a pretty path leading towards the shore in a different direction from the town. Curious about it, I went ahead.

There were pink roses on each side of the path, and when they ended, I came out onto a vast and long shore. At first, I thought there was no one there, but then in the distance, I saw what looked like a female figure in a black dress.

I walked closer to the ocean, which was gently and calmly washing back and forth on the sand. I was reluctant to walk towards the woman, for I myself knew the importance of having privacy, but the way she stood there gazing into the distance made me curious, so I began to slowly walk toward her.

Suddenly a large seagull flew very close to me and startled me. I almost tripped. When I regained balance and watched him fly off, I turned back to look at the woman, but she was no longer there! She was nowhere to be seen on this vast and wide shore! I could not believe she had disappeared from sight so quickly, and I thought the worst. I ran towards the water and frantically searched for her among the waves, but there was no one in the water. I was there a long time, perhaps too long, for the sun began to set, and I had to hurry back through the rose path and onto the stony street of the town.

Lights from the cafes and shops and the windows of houses twinkled in the twilight. I could hear softly playing guitars, laughter, and quiet, animated conversations.

I found a bench near a café called Manda and sat down. Its red door was open, and tables inside and out were filled with people drinking wine and talking. On a chair by the door was a man in a small black hat and a white shirt playing his guitar, his expression serene, lost in passion for the music. Meat was roasting on an open brazier. I relaxed, watching them. The lady from the shore was still on my mind, but I felt less anxious now as I drank in the atmosphere.

A young server asked if I needed a drink, and I chose one from the menu. It was pink, like the roses, with a hint of alcohol.

"Well, well, day one, and already couldn't resist coming back into our charming town."

Alain's voice came from my left. Dressed in all black, he was leaning on a wall and smiling. I nodded and invited him to sit with me.

"Is every night like this here?"

"Oh yes. Except for Sunday. People here are very religious."

"I'll have to find a suitable church, I suppose."

He gave me his wry smile. "There are three in town, a good number of options for a small place."

I smiled. "Tell me, do you play the guitar too?"

"Ah, you saw how I watch him play. No, I do

not. I enjoy it very much, the sound of it. It's very soothing. Even after all these years and countless nights, it's still soothing." Abruptly, Alain stood up. "I actually have to go, Ida, but I hope we meet again soon. I could take you on my boat and give you a tour around the island."

"Oh yes, I'd love that. You have a good night, Alain."

When he left, I had a mixed feeling of wanting him to stay and actually enjoying my time absorbing the atmosphere alone. I wasn't sure which I preferred at the moment. The server came back, but I only asked for water this time. I had to make sure I wasn't off balance when walking back home. I needed to get on my way. Fatigue was settling in, and I was thinking of that cozy, soft bed.

I slowly got up, and a few people smiled at me and waved goodbye as I began to walk back up the stone paved street towards the mansion. I felt my stride slowing down and becoming shorter. I remembered the way, but it would take a long time if I dragged like this. I mentally shook myself and was determined to speed up. I would have plenty of time in the coming days and weeks to explore the surroundings more.

As I reached the final path toward the house, I was up high above most of the town and the shore. I looked into the distance toward the lighthouse. Its light was spinning and blinking in a rhythm. Each time the light came around, I thought I could see the silhouette of someone standing by the railing. I remembered the name Alain had mentioned — Reficul Raul, the man who took care of the lighthouse, a farm, and a windmill. Perhaps he often looked out into the dark ocean, but for some strange reason, I felt that his eyes were on me. How he could have seen me from that distance and with the shadows on the path, I could not think. I looked at the lighthouse for a few more moments and then headed up the path to the house.

Nigel was waiting at the gate for me with a worried expression. He didn't say much, but he escorted me to my room and showed me a rope attached to a bell in his room. All I had to do was pull on it, and he'd know to come immediately. He also showed me how to use the telephone to call the servants' house.

"Your   grandmother   was   considering

purchasing a dog for company and safety. You may want to do that," Nigel said as he left me to get ready for bed. I thanked him and locked the door to my room.

As I began to undress for a shower, I got the uncanny feeling that someone was watching me. I turned, my heart pounding, but all that was there was the portrait of the beautiful Eleanor. Were her eyes looking straight ahead? I could have sworn her gaze was off to the side the first time I examined the painting. I regarded her for a few minutes, then finished undressing in the large bathroom.

The warm water soothed and relaxed me, and I thought it would be nice to see my room as it would have looked in the old days. I found some candles in a drawer and lit one, placing it in a candlestick on the mantle. I carried it carefully to the nightstand next to the bed, turned off the lights, and cozied up in the bed under the blankets, letting my head sink into the wonderful soft pillow. I became drowsy quickly, my vision blurring as my eyes closed and my fatigue took over. Just before fully losing consciousness, I thought I saw the silhouette of a woman bend over and blow out the candle. It had to have been my imagination.

I slipped into a deep sleep filled with calm dreams, still waters, soft, colorful flowers, and joy.

I woke up much later than was my usual habit and slowly sat up. The sun was shining through the gap in the curtains. A very thin ray of light cut the air and lit up Eleanor's face on the painting. I glanced at the nightstand, and the candle was indeed almost as tall as when I lit it. Perhaps, almost unconsciously, I didn't realize I had blown it out. I got dressed, donning a simple all-white outfit.

Downstairs Nigel was already active, and as soon as I came down, he hurried up to me, his face filled with worry. I sat in a chair in one of the smaller sitting rooms, as he suggested.

"Lady Ida, I must tell you this. From now on, when you go out closer to dark, either I or another servant must go with you, or perhaps you prefer to pay a guard. I suggest we go with your grandmother's plan in getting some dogs as well."

His tone was very serious. "What is wrong, Nigel? What happened?"

"A murder in town last night! Horrible. We get news immediately from our sheriff's department and the newspaper as well. Your grandmother had good relationships with both, and I made sure to continue that."

"But was it like the other cases? Oh, no…those were missing persons."

Nigel's face grew even more concerned. "You already know about those, too. I'm sorry…and…this is the first known murder on the island in two years. How sad for you that it happened the day you arrived. It was a stabbing in the alley. A young musician was killed."

I digested this information. "Who will investigate?"

"Surely Sheriff Lindon will, but he is the one on the missing persons case too. Unfortunately, he is not too bright. Before passing away, your grandmother wanted to speak to Chief of Police Clum to offer to pay the salary of a good investigator from the mainland. I believe she already had a candidate in mind. Right now, I think we should be very careful and get some dogs. You need to be safe in the nighttime."

"Well, Nigel, that gives me a good deal to think about." I sat there thinking. I needed to focus on just one thing from all that panic and mumbling from Nigel. "Well, then let's look for some dogs today.

Did Grandmother have a breeder in mind?" I could at least do this, and I actually looked forward to having some pets.

"Yes. There is a breeder in Burg village. We will bring Mark as well. We have a carriage with horses."

My mouth opened in shock. "We have horses?"

"Oh yes, how could I forget? We have stables and a field for them, located behind the servants' house and a line of trees."

"Okay, Nigel. But first, I need some breakfast."

Nigel's eyes widened, and he looked even more panicked. "Heavens! How could I not offer you a meal first thing!"

I smiled. "Calm down, Nigel. I'm not going to waste away just yet."

He shook his head and ran off, calling orders on the way to other servants. In less than fifteen minutes, I was sitting down to a square waffle with strawberries on top, smoked salmon with poached eggs, and some greens. It was delicious, and the aroma of both coffee and tea filled me with happiness and comfort.

After I finished, Nigel and Mark were ready, and I followed them to the stables. Since there were no cars around here, a carriage was the next fanciest thing, and the one Grandma had was beautiful—shiny black with red trim, almost like from a fairy tale. I got in, and Mark and Nigel climbed to the driver's seat. Mark chirruped to the horses, and the carriage lurched into motion. I relaxed against the black leather seat with a pillow and gazed out the window.

At first, the road was smooth, but then it became increasingly bumpy. I could hear Nigel yelling frantic apologies. Poor man, he was so high-strung. But perhaps that's what it took to be a top butler.

The scenery was beautiful. All around me were evergreen trees, and I could see colorful birds flitting about, and even a deer now and then with full antlers.

When the carriage stopped at our destination, Nigel jumped down to help me out, apologizing profusely. I was secretly amused. There was no use trying to tell him his concerns were unfounded.

Mark tied the horses to a hitching post and led us to a farmhouse standing among the trees. In the distance, I could see many more homes. So this was Burg.

A tall, muscular man in his forties met us at the front door. To say that he lacked any manners would be an understatement. He said nothing but looked me up and down, his face impassive. Nevertheless, I felt good energy coming from him as he led us around to the back of his property. There behind a fence in a large kennel were several Doberman pinschers. I was shaken at first because these dogs always seemed dangerous to me, but then I realized that no breed was better for home defense.

As the breeder, Nol, entered the penned space, the dogs joyfully barked and ran to him. He selected two of them, put them on leads, and brought them to us. "These two are brother and sister," he said in his gruff, deep voice. "The girl is Shell," he indicated the smaller of the two, "and this fellow is Knight. They are two years old and well-trained."

The dogs sat obediently next to Nol as he indicated that I should come over and offer each of them my closed fist to sniff. They did the same with Mark and Nigel. Nol told me to call them over, and they trotted to my side and sat, watching me with intelligent faces for their next order.

"I have been training these two, especially

for your grandmother," Nol said. He asked me to schedule a couple of dates over the next few weeks to give me more instructions and, I suspected, to see how his animals were being cared for.

I paid him, and we walked back to the carriage. Mark threw a large bag of food onto the luggage rack, the dogs gracefully leaped up into the carriage, and I followed. They calmly sat with me, watching me and pricking up their ears at the wildlife outside the windows. I felt nervous, but I ventured to pet them, and they offered me their backs to scratch. They seemed to accept me as their mistress and posed no threat to me. I smiled as I listened to their happy pants and scratched their backsides.

We arrived home well past the regular lunchtime, and I decided just to skip it and have an early dinner. Nigel and Mark assured me they would set up everything for the dogs inside the mansion. I thanked them and wandered out to sit in the garden and relax.

I sat in the wooden chair next to the garden table. All around me was the scent of flowers, and I watched the bees and butterflies go about their business. Mark brought out some tea for me. So this was how my grandmother was able to take on serious responsibilities for the town and to help everyone; she was able to balance it by having such peaceful places and moments. Did I have to pick up where she left off?

I felt that I had to continue her work on this island. I thought about the investigator Nigel had spoken of and immediately decided I had to wait longer, although what was I waiting for? What was holding me back? Perhaps those problems were past. That was my thought, or rather my hope. I leaned back and decided that first, I would speak to the chief of police, Clum, and after that, possibly the mayor, Konig.

Mark appeared again with a copy of the island's only newspaper for me. Eagerly I read the front page. The headline was dedicated to a certain Professor Guud. This scientist was apparently making a breakthrough in curing various diseases and illnesses, and from what I read, he was dedicated to the poor in the community and constantly helping those in need and those who struggled.

I wondered if my grandmother had known him well also. Perhaps he was a good contact to make if I were going to get involved and continue in Grandma's footsteps.

The rest of the day, I spent in peace and quiet observation, mostly alone with my own thoughts. As the night came on, I once again was in my room with a candle lit and the lights off. From time to time, I could hear the dogs walk by in the hallway outside my room, their claws clicking on the wood floor. I wondered whether they were restless, perhaps simply getting used to the new house or patrolling it. I lay down, watching the candle burn. The flicker of the ever-changing flame calmed me.

Suddenly I thought I heard human footsteps right outside my door. I sat up quickly and, at the same time, heard the dogs bark and run down the hall. I grabbed the candle and opened the door.

The dogs came to me and sat next to me protectively. They seemed calm now, and I did not notice anything suspicious. From time to time, they both would look at the window at the end of the hallway. I walked over to it and looked out.

The moon was bright, and it illuminated the garden and made the flowers seem cold blue in color. Suddenly my heart began to pound as I noticed a woman in a black dress standing among the flowers. She turned toward the house and seemed to look right at me. Eleanor Blackswan! How could that be? I shook my head and shut my eyes in fear. When I ventured to look outside again, there was no longer anyone there. The dogs were at my feet, looking up at me with concern. I went back to my room and opened the door for the dogs, encouraging them to come inside. I never would have thought I'd want them to sleep in my room, but I was so frightened I wanted them as close as possible. They lay down on the soft carpet at the foot of the bed.

I held the candle close to the painting of Eleanor, scanning it carefully. Once again, it looked as though her eyes had moved. Was my mind playing tricks on me? Was seeing her out there in the garden just the wild imagination of an overwhelmed mind? I got back in bed, blew out the candle, and lay down.

CHAPTER THREE

The next several days were rather uneventful, and I was grateful for it. I spent the entire time in the house and the garden. I read books of poetry and sat by the fireplace drinking tea at night. My every need was answered by the servants. It was nice to live the life of a great lady.

Finally, I decided to go back to the town once all my thoughts were gathered. One morning I set out alone, despite protests from Nigel, and walked to the town.

The first thing I did was go to the lovely café and bakery La Dame Ava. As I entered, a young boy greeted me close to the entrance. He was holding a pretty white cat.

I squinted at the cat, then addressed the boy. "So, is this Ava?"

"Yes, miss."

"And you are?"

"Misha."

"He is our most important helper and our son." I heard a voice to my right, and a man with blond hair just like the boy's came from behind the counter. "My name is Thomas." Then he pointed at the woman who had just appeared behind the counter with platters of more freshly baked cookies and pastries. "That is Margaret. We run and own this place. We were told you came by the other day. Someone was covering for us. You are Ida Clifton, aren't you?"

I smiled. "Yes indeed. Did you know my grandmother?"

His face took on a sad smile. "Your grandmother bailed us out during hard financial times. She was our saint. I am very happy to see you here now. You are always welcome here, Lady Ida."

I blushed. The more I found out about my grandmother, the more I realized how little I actually knew of her generous nature and heart of gold. Tears gathered in my eyes. "Thank you."

"Ah, you are hungry, of course. Please, please, take a seat. Everything is fresh here. You just tell me what you'd like."

I sat by the window with a nice view of the pretty street. It was slowly starting to come to life. I ordered a coffee and a plate of bread samples with butter and berries. As I enjoyed my breakfast, I thought about the social life and friends I had left behind, along with other family members. Would I be able to make friends here? Real friends, not just people who had admired my grandmother. I wished my parents could be with me, but sadly my father had suffered a terrible accident and became paralyzed from the waist down, and ever since then, my mother had been taking care of him. It was tough. Perhaps I could bring them here. I was surely going to send them a good deal of money. I felt like a bad daughter at times, filling my life with studies, work, and friends. I always went against the norms. Because I looked much younger than my true age, most thought I was too young to settle down, But once they found out I was thirty-three and unmarried, their expressions were shocked, sometimes even horrified. Oh well, I had learned to ignore it and keep going. I did want a family, children, and a man, but I was not desperate. I wanted someone I would truly love. I believed and had faith. Perhaps my next step was waiting here on this island, the place to contemplate and answer so many questions.

When I finished, I said my goodbyes to the pleasant family and headed towards the harbor. Once there, I saw a familiar face. To my surprise, Gonzalo was still on the island — or should I say back on the island. He was loading something on a boat, which I recognized as Alain's ship. It looked like Alain had given Gonzalo a job. This was a kind and generous move. With my eyes, I searched for Alain.

"Well, well, out and about." I heard Alain's voice behind me. He was carrying a box. "I'll be right with you, Ida. Just let me load this one up."

"I'll be right here."

After he loaded it and spoke to Gonzalo, he came back to me. I saw Gonzalo wave at me, and I waved back.

"I know a great place where we can talk," said Alain.

"I'd love to see it."

The building Alain led me to stood on the street that fronted the harbor and looked rather ridiculous. It resembled a large red barn. Above it hung a plank with its name, Horseshoe Tavern.

Alain grinned at my startled gaze. "Not much on the outside, but the father and son who run this, Hubert and Bibo, are amazing chefs and take excellent care of their customers. They are great fishermen as well."

The inside was simple but very clean. Everything was wooden, with red cloths on the tables. Immediately a young, chubby man approached us and, with a big smile, showed us to a table with a view of the water.

Alain recommended their house special drink for me, tea with milk. I told Alain that I had eaten already, but the drink would be fine and that I didn't mind if he ate. He ordered tea as well. When we told the young man, Bibo, that we'd only have drinks, he seemed disappointed, but Alain assured him we'd be back sometime for lunch or dinner.

"So, how has your first week on the island gone so far, Ida?"

I lifted my shoulders and spread my hands.

"Well, what can I say, Alain? My mind is completely full. I've been a bit overwhelmed by the pace, but I think I've been able to slow down and reorganize my thoughts. I suppose starting in a new place is always a lot to handle, but here it's especially a lot. And then the murder put everyone at the mansion on edge."

"Oh yes...." Alain shook his head. "It's shocking. I've told you about rumors of creatures that take people. You saw the sailors vanish with your own eyes. But what happened the other night is completely different. We all have to be cautious at night until it's resolved."

Worry creased my forehead. "Do you think the police will be able to handle it?"

"Probably."

Our drinks came, and indeed the homegrown tea and milk were delicious; it was a good recommendation. Outside, seagulls gathered on the pier, waiting to steal some food from fishermen.

"I wonder what my grandmother would do in this situation."

Alain thought for a moment. "Well, she'd probably try to keep everyone calm. At least that's my guess."

When we finished, Alain offered to walk with me around the harbor before he had to get back to work. As we walked, he told me short stories about the various workers and fishermen at the docks. There were many colorful and splendid characters, and Alain kept me laughing. It seemed like a community with a lot of strength, positivity, and strong will. He then walked me to the path leading back to the mansion and said he had to go back to help Gonzalo. Before he left, I got information about Mayor Konig and headed to his house.

When I arrived, I had to double-check the address to make sure I was correct, for it was a humble, small townhouse between two others in the middle of an ordinary street. I knocked on the door, and shortly a stout bald man with a pleasant smile appeared. He wore an unremarkable brown suit that barely fit him.

"Mayor Konig?"

"That is correct, miss. And you are? Is this urgent? I will be heading to the town hall soon."

"I'm Ida Clifton. I just wanted to talk to you. I figured you knew my grandmother."

The man's plump hands flew to his cheeks.

"Oh my goodness! Come in, please! So happy to meet you!"

His home was as humble looking as he was. His wife came out to greet me. She, too, seemed to be a very simple woman, but she didn't seem to want to stick around and cheerfully went upstairs with her coffee. I felt that perhaps I was disturbing them. Mayor Konig showed me to a table, and we sat down. He offered tea or coffee, and I thanked him and accepted a cup, mainly to be polite.

"So, Ida, you like our island? What brings you to my home today? I spoke to your grandmother often."

I smiled. "The island is wonderful."

I decided not to tell the mayor about the terrible things that had happened at the beginning of my journey here, even though I figured he knew already.

I set down my cup and leaned toward the mayor. "I learned about certain plans my grandmother had and was wondering what you'd think of them."

"Please do tell me."

"It's about the missing people, but perhaps now with the murder too...."

He looked somber. "Murders."

I drew back, startled. "What do you mean?"

"There was a second one, also with a knife, the same, what do they say, modus operandi. But we were able to keep it quiet in order not to cause total panic."

I sucked in my breath. "Oh no, this presses matters then. " My grandmother, before she died, found an investigator from the mainland who was willing to come here to the island. Now, I would be willing to become his official employer and pay him to come here to investigate. I just did not want to override any authority, and I would like to have your approval for this." I gazed at him in what I hoped was a humble, supplicating way.

The mayor rubbed his chin and gazed out the window. "I'll be honest with you." He hung his head as his tone became hopeless. "Our police are not cut out for this. They are not the brightest, but they think they are. If you were to do this for us, it would be a very good thing, Ida."

My mind was made up. "Then I shall try and contact this investigator immediately."

"Thank you, Ida. And if you need any help from me, please let me know, and tell him this as well." We stood and shook hands, and I left the little house.

I was feeling better about my plans, and I headed back to the mansion with the intention to follow through first thing, but I was chilled to learn about the second murder. The possibility of a serial killer on the island was high now.

When I arrived at my gate, I saw a crew of men working on the trees and in the field. Nigel hurried out of the house, so he had probably been watching for me.

"I'm so sorry, Lady Ida. I forgot to mention that a crew comes every two weeks and takes care of the grass and the trees! Oh, and Nella is here right now. She brought you some herbal teas that she made herself."

"Thank you, Nigel. I need to make an urgent call, but please, could you brew me one of her teas and thank her for me?"

"Of course!"

He went to complete his task while I headed upstairs, found the contact's information, and sat down next to the telephone.

Once I completed the call, my tea was brought

by the lovely Michelle. Her face was clouded, and she seemed not to be in the best mood.

"Would you like to join me for tea, Michelle?" I asked, gesturing to the nearest chair.

She looked startled by the question. I was quick to convince her to sit down, and I poured a cup for her.

"What is troubling you, Michelle? Is it something I can help with?"

Michelle looked down at her lap. "It's just silly things, Lady Ida. The man I went out with last night left a bad feeling with me. At first, he was nice, but when I refused to go with him after dinner at the café, he got very pushy, and almost became violent, even. He grabbed my arm tightly, but luckily there were still people around."

This disturbed me more than I let on. "Oh no, I'm so sorry! I think we all need to make sure we do not go out alone from now on until safety is restored. I have a man coming in two days. He is an experienced criminal investigator. He will be staying here in the house, in the first-floor guest room. I will be paying him very well, and I hope he will resolve the matters of the murder and disappearances."

Michelle looked very relieved. "Thank you, I am very grateful."

She seemed a little uncomfortable trying to make small talk with the mistress of the house, and though I felt she hadn't told me everything that was bothering her, I didn't want to press the issue and let her go on about her work.

Well, at least I was doing what I could. In a few days, I was going to go to the harbor to fetch the man who could actually do something to help the inhabitants of this island. With luck, nothing more would happen until then.

I was so wrong.

CHAPTER FOUR

As the night was slowly setting in, I turned on a lot of lights in the house. Both dogs were lying on a soft sheepskin downstairs by the fireplace, chewing on bones and enjoying the warmth. I joined them, sitting on a cozy soft couch next to the fireplace with tea in hand.

As it got later, the wind outside began to increase, and a storm blew in. I could hear some branches scratching on one of the windows. Knight raised his head, alert. He trotted over to the window and stared out for a while, and once he understood the noise, he came back to his comfortable spot next to his sister, Shell.

The lights in the room across the hall were

off, and I could see the outline of a tree outside the window, illuminated from time to time by lightning strikes. Then a streak of lightning showed what looked like the silhouette of a person standing by the window. I almost spilled my remaining tea as I jumped up, startled. I placed the cup on the table. Both dogs were up on their feet and looking in the same direction. So they had seen it too! There was someone in the house! My heart began to pound, and my hands shook as I frantically wondered if I should run to the bell pull and ring for the servants or simply stay in this spot and rely on these strong dogs alone. I stared into the other room but no longer could see any signs of a person.

The dogs then ran forward and stopped in front of the staircase. They both began to growl, their attention fixed on something up the stairs. I timidly and with fearful, slow steps walked over and stood beside them. I tried to see what they saw, and when lightning again illuminated the window, I saw a silhouette, this time by the tall mirror close to my grandparents' portraits. The dogs barked loudly and sprinted up the stairs but then looked confused as they stopped next to the mirror. As I walked up after them, I could not see anyone.

And then I saw the door to my room wide open. Chills ran down my spine as I slowly followed the dogs as they rushed into the room. I turned on the lights with my shaking hand. Everything seemed normal — until I looked into the mirror.

I screamed and fell back, ending up sitting on the floor. In the mirror stood a beautiful but pale Eleanor Blackswan. Her lips were moving, but there was no sound. The dogs were barking at the mirror, and I was motionless, watching it in terror, and then Eleanor was gone, and only my reflection appeared as I stood up.

The rest of the night I spent by the fireplace downstairs with a large blanket and the dogs close by, but I barely slept. Had it been real? Or was fatigue and stress crushing my mind and senses? Oh God, I prayed so much that night.

When morning came, I finally fell asleep, completely exhausted.

I woke up around noon with the dogs nosing me in the face. I was surprised that they hadn't roused me earlier, but Nigel informed me that he had taken them out for some exercise so I could rest.

Tactfully skirting the issue of my night spent on the sofa, Nigel asked what I'd like to eat, and despite it no longer being early morning, I asked him for coffee and breakfast.

Chef Daniel was quickly on the case. A perfect omelet with onions and tomatoes and a croissant on the side were shortly served. I was still uneasy after the night's experience and could not fully enjoy the food; I ate rather quickly. I screwed up my courage and resolutely went back up the stairs again to my room and stood in front of the mirror. It looked completely normal, but I asked Nigel to take it down into the basement. He asked if I wanted to replace it with another, but I declined.

I changed my clothes, did my hair, and requested Mark to take me on a carriage ride into the Everett region. As we wound along the road away from the town, we passed beautiful green fields, some leading up into the hills and some stretching down in the direction of the ocean. From time to time, I saw children playing, horses running, and dogs sniffing about. There were several large farmhouses, and on the bend around a hill, I could see a large flock of sheep. The black sheepdog seemed to smile as he enjoyed harassing them. On the very top of the hill, I could see the shepherd watching over them.

The road dipped down and led toward the smaller town described to me as a fishermen's village, but its official name was Everett. On the right side of the town, far in the distance, I could see the windmill and the lighthouse and the small farm that were visible from Cristium.

When we stopped, I asked Mark if it was safe to go all the way to the lighthouse. He assured me that it was, but he also said it was advisable to ride horses there, for there was no road wide enough for the carriage.

The town of Everett looked a bit dark and gloomy. There were barely any people out and about, but in the bay, I could see several fishermen gathering. It did not look like a place I would enjoy, but I was very curious about the lighthouse, and I let Mark know that I was an experienced horseback rider.

Mark arranged some blankets in place of saddles and boosted me up onto a powerful black horse. Mark followed me on the smaller grey one. We rode at a quiet, peaceful pace, but it felt so wild and freeing. The ocean breeze blew my hair up as we rode across a field and soon arrived near the little farm.

Closer up, the lighthouse was massive. I finally understood how tall and big it was, and as I gazed up at it in wonder, I failed to notice the man who walked up to us.

"Excuse m-m-m-mee." I heard a stuttering, thin voice.

I turned to my right, and there stood a timid-looking man in red pants and a white shirt. He ducked his head, and his entire posture became timid. He had large black eyes and messy black hair, and his mouth was missing a few teeth.

"A-a-are yu-u-uo in ne-eed of heaalp?"

I nearly laughed, to my shame. I smiled widely and breathed deeply to gain some composure. Then I held out my hand. "I am Ida Clifton. I wanted to come and look at the lighthouse."

"Ye-yesss, I am Ra-raul. I'll le-lead yu-you to the l-l-lighthouse...."

I was astonished that this was Reficul Raul. But since he had introduced himself only as Raul, that was what I decided to call him.

Raul waved us to follow him as he limped past the farmhouse and headed toward a narrow path to the lighthouse. The steps were wide, and so was the black iron door. I could see the waves crashing below us unto the cliffs. Raul opened the door with a struggle. This was the man Alain had described as very capable, and who did a lot of work in the area? I suppose slow and steady really did win the race, as I imagined Raul had to work tirelessly to accomplish much with his physical limitations and perhaps mental as well. Then I shook my head, knowing better than to pass judgement like this. I followed him in. Mark was right behind me. Raul pointed towards the top but shook his finger.

"Thaaat is, is w-way up, but I-I, p-p-painted it this m-m-morning. B-b-black paint. M-ma-maybe can gooo up...next v-visit."

He smiled, showing his crooked and missing teeth, and nodded, waiting for approval. I nodded reluctantly but thanked him for showing us this far, and we left to get back home before dark.

As we rode back to the carriage and then headed home, I went over the encounter with Raul. It was strange, to say the least. I still wondered about the praise Alain had heaped on him. Perhaps there was much more than met the eye with this man.

Back home, Nigel had gotten everything ready for dinner, and the dish of the day was freshly caught whitefish grilled with tomatoes and asparagus, with roasted pears on the side. In a separate bowl came rice sprinkled with fresh cilantro. It was all accompanied with black tea with a slice of lemon. I picked the lemon out, and Nigel immediately took note. Tea was a bit too sour for me if the lemon remained in the cup for long.

I invited Nigel to dine with me, and he refused, almost with shock on his face. I laughed and slowly enjoyed my delicious meal.

Outside, the sun was setting, and dark clouds gathered once again. It reminded me of the previous night. I felt uncomfortable. I hoped with all my heart that no trouble would manifest itself tonight. There was no way I could reveal my concerns to Nigel. He would think I was mentally unbalanced. And I wasn't sure whether it was just my nerves playing tricks on me, despite the dogs' behavior.

I relaxed on the couch after the meal. I tried to clear my mind of all negative thoughts and closed my eyes, and before I knew it, I was asleep. I found myself standing on the edge of cold stony cliffs. On my left towered the massive lighthouse. The waves brutally crashed into the shore. On my right, I heard voices in the distance. There were people all in black gathering on the shore. Behind them on the hill stood a young woman in a black dress. She was calling to them and motioning them to come back. It was the beautiful Eleanor!

They did not listen to her. One after another, they entered the sea and disappeared in the waves. This continued until none remained. Eleanor ran down to the shore and fell to her knees. Then she pounded on the sand with her fists, screaming and crying in horror and anguish. I could feel her pain. She turned her face to me and reached out her hand.

Abruptly I opened my eyes and sat up. The two Dobermans slightly raised their heads and looked at me as they lay by the fireplace. The house was quiet, but I could hear the wind gathering power outside. Then followed the rain.

"Is that what really happened to the Blackswans? Did she just show me? In my dreams?" I said aloud. The dogs looked at me with questioning faces.

I was confused. Was such a thing possible? I had to find someone who knew more. I had to visit the local library.

Though it wasn't too late, I hesitated to call Nigel but decided I needed to talk to him. "Nigel, do we have any books about local history and the families who lived here?"

"Yes, indeed, ma'am. I will bring it presently." Nigel left and was soon back with a book with a black leather binding. Stamped in gold was the title, *Paradise Shores History*.

I stayed awake for hours, reading the book and drinking cups of tea until I couldn't keep my eyes open. I finally went up to my room with the dogs. I did not light a candle and even avoided looking at Eleanor's painting, which I felt was watching me. Thank God I was able to sleep without trouble this night.

CHAPTER FIVE

When I woke, I realized the investigator I had hired was arriving today. I rushed to get dressed in a green outfit and then had a very light breakfast—just a coffee and some cut-up fruit.

Nigel accompanied me to the harbor, as it was still quite early, and he was protective to the point of being paranoid. I told him there was no need for him to go, but he insisted, and I knew arguing was fruitless.

The town wasn't coming to life, as usual, this morning, for it was Sunday, and on this day, most people stayed in or went to church, and most businesses and cafés were closed. As we walked down the stony path, in the distance, I could see thick fog over the ocean, and it was impossible to know if the ship was close or had come into port already.

We hurried to the main long pier, where I could see the silhouette of a man in a long black coat and a top hat of the same color against the gray fog. He had his back turned toward us, looking out into the foggy sea.

I ordered Nigel to stay at the end of the pier and walked down the wharf toward the man alone. His eyebrow lifted, but he didn't argue. It was chilly, and I shivered in my light skirt and green jacket. I folded my arms and walked quickly with my head down.

When I lifted my head, the man was facing me and was just a few meters away. I was shocked to see how youthful he appeared, considering that in the profile she left, Grandma had noted that he was in his forties. He looked no more than thirty-five, had sharp but relaxed features, and his eyes were green and keen. Straight away, he gave off the aura of a man who missed no details.

"I suppose you are my employer. Ida Clifton?" he said in a calm, deep voice, lifting his hat.

"Yes, that is correct. Investigator Nistage." I

put out my hand to shake his. "It's good to welcome you here."

"Just Luc, please, and the pleasure is all mine." He stooped down to pick up only one suitcase. I was surprised to see how little he had brought with him.

I suppose my confusion must have shown on my face, and I was briefly rooted to the spot. Luc smiled as if he were greatly amused and said, "Shall we talk more here? Do you find this spot comfortable?"

I felt myself blush to the roots of my hair. "Oh, no, no, please follow me. Let's get you to the estate, where you can rest, and then we can talk." I gestured toward Nigel.

"Rest...." Again, the amused smile. "I've had too much rest, but I suppose a little more won't hurt."

I decided not to ask any questions.

Luc greeted Nigel with a short and respectful line, but he did not inquire who Nigel was. It was probably pretty obvious. Nigel offered to carry the suitcase, but Luc shook his head with a smile.

He asked a few short and general questions about the town and surroundings and looked around appraisingly as we walked to the mansion, saying he would want to know more later. When we got to the gate, the dogs came barreling toward us.

"Sit!" I commanded, and Luc offered his closed fist to each animal to sniff. I told them this man was a friend, and they trotted obediently into the house before us.

I showed Luc into the ground-floor guest room, and we agreed to talk at lunch. Though I was anxious, at the same time, I felt encouraged by his calm, confident demeanor.

When Nigel announced that lunch was served, Luc came into the room in simple black slacks and a white shirt. He wore no watch, and he looked a bit less intimidating without the hat.

He sat on my right at the table. Mark served the roasted chicken with vegetables. Nigel already knew all my preferences, and now he stood above Luc. "What would you like to drink, Mr. Nistage?"

"Just Luc, please. Black tea, and keep it coming if possible, thank you."

"I like tea as well." I smiled.

Yes, I am a regular black tea drinker. I was a regular whiskey drinker also, but I finally was able to give it up."

"How long ago?" I asked, sipping a glass of

water.

"I have not had any alcohol in five years," he said, twisting his own water glass by the stem.

I was a bit surprised. "Not even a sip of wine?"

Luc grinned ruefully. "No. A sip can lead to more sips, more sips to half a glass, half a glass to a full one...and then it's the whole bottle before you know it." He looked as though he were going to say more but stopped.

"So, Luc, why did you agree to come here when other investigators, according to my grandmother, had no interest?" I asked, cutting into my chicken. "Can you tell me more about your experience?"

Luc swallowed a bite of roasted peppers, then said, "I'm surprised others declined, considering the generous pay, although money has nothing to do with my decision. It was about a challenge... redemption...a feeling inside...and it was this island's name."

"Paradise Shores?"

"Yes. My most harrowing case—and one that changed my life—took place in a town called Paradise Harbor. I spent several years in prison because a dissatisfied client wanted to punish me."

Luc shrugged, looking down at his plate. "But I understood him. When I got out, I was in my thirties. I had hidden some money, a good sum, and was able to get a house. Years I spent just...well, wasting time, but then I faced my fears and became an investigator again. It's been ten years now since I re-started my career. I have not failed in a single investigation since then. Prior to Paradise Harbor, I had not failed, either."

His words were intriguing. "Would you tell me more about that case? That sounds devastating but also inspiring. You seem to have overcome a lot."

He snorted. "Right now, I'd rather talk about the situation here. I'll tell you more about my experience in the future."

"All right then," I said primly. "What do you think about the initial things I told you?"

Luc leaned back and placed his napkin on the table. "Well, first thing, we cannot rule out that the disappearances and the murders are the demented work of the same person. Someone could have simply changed his or her pattern. I'll have to do a lot of research. Visit archives, and explore all the areas on the island."

"And I'll be going with you."

He frowned, staring at my face for what seemed to be a long time, but he knew I was his employer. "Well, why not? That is not how I usually work, but until I know more, we can investigate together. Who did this house belong to before your grandparents? How long was it empty before they purchased it?"

It was my turn to frown at him. "How do you know it has not been in my family for generations?"

"The walls, floors, stairs, everything has been rebuilt. You do need experience to notice this, but don't worry, it's not obvious."

"It was a family named Blackswan."

"And where are they now?"

"No one is sure what happened to them."

Luc tapped a forefinger against his temple. "That is never true. Someone does know. Finding that someone and getting him to talk...that's the thing. Blackswan.... You mentioned the crew who disappeared from the shipwreck. Is there any description of the creature they believe is around here?"

"Not that I know of," I said with a shrug.

"Well, we will have to find out, Ida. Hmm. It'll

be dangerous."

He stared at me again, deep into my eyes. I lifted my chin and stared back, trying to show him I had no fear of danger, but inside I was shaking.

Luc suddenly got up from the table and went into his room, then emerged with a small gun and a box. He walked over to me and placed both next to my plate, then went back to his seat. Chills ran down my spine, but again I tried to show him I was comfortable, and I smiled while looking at the gun. He laughed.

"Ida, it's normal to feel nervous, even scared. Allow yourself the emotions. Just don't let them control you. I'll teach you how to use that," he said, nodding at the gun. "It's my extra gun. I usually hide it on my body when I go into dangerous places, but now, since I'll have you as my partner, my revolver will work just fine, and you'll be safer knowing how to use that."

I relaxed a little. "Yes, thank you. But why do you think it'll be dangerous?"

"Ha!" He gave a short, mirthless laugh. "Well, the creature, or creatures, if we run into them, will probably not be friendly. And whoever is stabbing people in the streets of this peaceful-looking place won't be very happy to see us, either." Luc shook his head. "I feel that a storm is hiding here." Then he stood. "Thank you for the lunch. Please get ready to go with me to the library and town archives next."

Luc inclined his head at me and went to his room. I exhaled slowly. It was a lot for me to handle, but I was clearly lucky to have such a man working for me. I told myself I was ready for whatever was to come. I had chosen this path and could neither blame nor involve anyone else.

I went upstairs, and as I took my time changing into a fresh and comfortable outfit, I watched the painting of Eleanor. She seemed alive, as usual, her eyes bright in the rays of the sun coming from the window.

After I got dressed, I went into the bathroom and looked at myself in the mirror. Realization struck me. I looked quite a bit like Eleanor! No. No, something was happening inside my brain; my head was filled with confusion. I went downstairs, where Luc was already waiting. He was leaning on the stair railing with his legs crossed, once again wearing the long black coat and the hat.

"Let's go and dig in," he said, smirking.

Nigel opened the door and looked nervous as we left. Luc spoke to me, sotto voce, as the door closed behind us. "A big worry man, that one... seems to have a good heart too. It's all right."

I laughed a little. "Yes, he loved my grandma very much, and he's very overprotective."

"Can't say I blame him, considering what's been happening on this island."

As we went down the street and turned the corner, Luc looked back at La Dame Ava Café with interest. "Nice place?"

Nodding enthusiastically, I replied, "It is wonderful. Run by a family my grandmother helped in the past, very nice people."

"Ah. I'll go there sometime."

"Ida!" I heard a voice behind me. It was Alain, coming from a side street. "Good to see you! Is everything going well?" Alain smiled and nodded toward Luc.

I hurried to make introductions. "Everything is well, Alain. This is investigator Luc Nistage. My grandmother was going to hire him before her passing. He's here to help us with the situation."

"Oh, well...that is great indeed. Nice to meet you, Mr. Nistage." Alain's face betrayed no concern or even interest.

Luc gave his little formal head bow. "Just Luc, please. Are you a friend of the family?"

"I helped Ida out with a few things when she got here."

I jumped in. "Alain is the man who took us back to the ship, the situation I told you about."

"Ah yes, yes, that's right. That is fortunate! Well...um, we do have to go, yes?"

"Oh, I'm sorry, I won't be holding you up. Let's talk more soon, Ida. Nice to meet you, Luc!" Alain smiled and walked off after waving one more time.

Luc turned to me, concern on his face. "Don't rush to trust anyone, okay?"

What? Alain was a friend, not a foe! "But he helped me. He's very nice!"

Luc shook his head. "Smiles, politeness, helpfulness—all this does not make someone trustworthy. Just be careful with private information, that's all."

"That is your professional advice, then?" I challenged, somewhat irritated.

The investigator was unruffled. "That's correct. The library is just up ahead."

He remained cool and calm as we came up to a large, by this town's standards, red building. This housed the library and the archives of the entire island. We hoped to find some useful information here about ancestral families and also perhaps even clues as to whom we could speak to next.

The air inside was rather stuffy, and the filled bookshelves reached all the way to the rather low ceiling. It wasn't as well-lit as a library should be.

From the small desk on the right, an older woman approached us. She had long grey hair and narrow reading glasses and introduced herself as Ruth. Her air, as that of most librarians, was rather proprietary, and she definitely gave us the feeling that if we stepped out of line in any way, we would be banished, never to be allowed back in. It made me feel like a twelve-year-old again.

Luc and I smiled conspiratorially, and he pointed out a sign showing the way to the archive section. We sat at a table, and Luc put a pile of documents in front of me with a small stack of scrap paper to use as markers, with instructions to mark anything I found about the Blackswans, while he himself was going to focus on specific events. What those events were, he did not say.

At first, it was exciting, but after an hour, it began to feel like torture as I turned page after page. Luc, however, seemed to be having a much better time than I was. He was absorbed in his reading, going from paper to paper, and from time to time, smiling about something he had found.

This went on for another two hours. Luc slapped together the last archive document and informed me that he was done, but just for today. He had also read the papers and documents I marked and made pages of notes. He then checked out a book written by Theodore Blackswan called *Life in Paradise*.

At home, Luc asked me to sit with him near the fireplace. We took seats across from each other with the dogs lying on the floor between us.

"Here is what we have so far, Ida. First of all, people have been disappearing in this place since the last century. I found evidence in old papers and documents. It seems to be happening more often now, and from the newer newspapers, I have concluded that there are increasing incidents of animal attacks around the island. However...." Luc paused, leaning forward and spreading his hands. "The animals were not identified, which means the authorities could not tell what kind of animal was attacking, and the survivors could not tell them, either.

"What does this mean? I theorize that these are not conventional beasts that we know. And the increase of incidents may mean that there are now more sources of the problem. But the difference between now and then is that the earlier disappearances were all related to the water, the ocean—not land-based attacks. Those are still happening, as you saw when the sailors disappeared. So, there are two problems."

Luc rubbed his brow. "About the knife murders. There is nothing I have turned up yet to shed any light on them. I will have to do some more snooping around and visit the other regions on the island. A certain Doctor Guud moved to this island just a few years ago, so we should talk to him soon. And lastly, about the Blackswans. What we know, so far, is that almost all of them disappeared in 1865. It was a very large family, and only two sisters, Eleanor and Mary and their brother Theodore remained. Mary left the island that year, and Theodore and

Eleanor stayed. Apparently, sometime after both of them disappeared also, but there is no sure date. The estate was legally in their names for a long time until your grandparents bought it. I reckon this book by Theodore Blackswan will help us to understand the island better." He leaned back in his seat. "So. Any questions?"

I pondered for a moment, trying to absorb all this information. "I wonder why Nigel didn't tell me these things. I was under the impression that he knew the estate well before my grandparents' time."

"Why would he tell you unless you asked? You should ask him. I can, too."

"I guess it is time we interviewed him."

"Good, good. After I read this book, maybe I'll get more clues, and tonight I will go out and get a feel of what it's like at night around here."

"I'll come too." I would be safe with Luc and his revolver.

"As you wish. Rest before then, since you can never know what will happen."

I thought about speaking to Nigel right then, but it was Michelle and Silvia who were doing the work around the house. I figured Nigel needed the time off, a rarity but good for his age. Out in the garden, I noticed Nella and decided to talk to her.

The old lady had her hands full of dirt as she was adding a mixture of compost around the plants. It was getting cooler with each day, but it was still relatively warm. It wouldn't get cold enough on the island to kill the plants as long as they were taken care of properly, which Nella clearly knew how to do.

I came up to her and spoke softly in order not to startle her. "Hello, Nella, how are you today? Would you tell me about what you are adding there?"

The older woman started to get up, but I motioned for her to stay in place and squatted down beside her.

"Oh, dear Lady Ida, I'm well. How about you?"

"I'm doing well. It's getting a bit colder these days, but it's still warm compared to where I came from."

"Yes, that is why I have to do this. I am adding a mix for the plants to sustain them. It's loamy soil mixed with several ingredients. Pine bark helps the soil to filter oxygen and nutrients. I also add alfalfa, lime, and kelp. Sometimes wood ash is also added, but not this time."

I was impressed. "You have so much knowledge on this subject! It's incredible."

"Just many years of experience, darling. You'd be just as good if this were your favorite pastime."

Nella smiled and continued. I wondered about her life. Did she have a family? Why was this her favorite thing to do? I thought of what I'd be like when I was older and grey like this. Would I have a family? I gazed around at the flowers. A beautiful red flower was at eye level with me. I relaxed my face and watched the pretty pattern of its petals without thinking of anything else.

Before long, I heard a familiar voice calling out to me. It was Alain. I got up and happily greeted him. To my pleasant surprise, he had come to invite me to dinner in town that night, and he promised live music. Though I had planned to go out with Luc, I agreed to dine with Alain.

Once back in the house, I slipped a note under Luc's door explaining that I was not going to join him as we had previously planned. Then I asked Michelle and Silvia to put the big cheval mirror back into my room. I decided I had to face that which was irrational and figure out what was happening in my mind.

After they left the room, I closed the door and began to choose an outfit for dinner. I settled on a black dress I had never worn before. As I began to undress, I felt someone's breath on my neck, and I quickly turned around. There was no one, just my own reflection in the mirror and the painting of Eleanor next to it. Her eyes, as usual, seemed to be looking at me. I knew this was a silly thought. I got closer to the mirror and examined my face, then hers. What was bothering me? I could not figure it out. However, I did not suffer the same visions as before, and that was a relief.

I extended my hand and touched Eleanor's face, and suddenly darkness appeared in front of my eyes. It was only for a moment, but when my vision cleared, I found myself touching my own reflection in the mirror. What was going on?

I left the room and spent the rest of the time waiting for Alain downstairs. Luc did not emerge from his room, and when Alain arrived, I left, wondering if Luc actually cared that I wouldn't be joining him for his nighttime investigation.

Alain looked charming, dressed in a perfectly tailored suit. He walked by my side with a gentle yet confident stride as he told me about our destination, a restaurant that featured live music. He said the island's best singer, Emmanuela, was performing tonight.

The sun slowly set, and as we walked down into the town on the stony path, I could see the final purple glow outlining the lighthouse in the distance.

"Alain, you told me about Raul before. I recently met him, and he didn't seem as capable as I imagined from what you said."

"There is a lot to Raul that doesn't meet the eye," Alain replied cryptically.

We turned down a side street, and he pointed to a place at the end. The staff was setting up tables outside, and a small wooden stage had been erected. Candles were lit as the final light of the day was gone, and night covered the sky with its dark blanket. We sat at a table close to the stage, and a waiter brought us two glasses, some thinly sliced cheese, and a bottle of fine wine.

The place was buzzing. Eventually, all the tables were filled, and some people stood with their backs against the walls of the restaurant. A few came out onto their balconies to enjoy the live music.

Emmanuela stepped onto the stage. She was a heavy-set woman in her forties, and as she began to sing, her charm filled the air. She had a smooth, controlled, and smoky voice. Alain sat there smiling at me as he saw my delight.

> "Far away, the shore is crying
> For the one who lost his way
> He was broken but undying,
> Eternity had her say
>
> Do you know this love undying?
> Too much life is no good,
> Do you know why you are crying?
> All those you loved misunderstood
>
> Far away they are in heaven,
> but you are still right here
> Wandering on the barren shores
>
> Was it eight years? Or seven?
> That I saw you last,

Oh, you poor soul, undying,
You cannot take your life

Far away they are in heaven
With a candle lit, you feel
Will you go there soon, to heaven?
You ask forever as you kneel."

Her song lyrics were very unusual: sad poems with hidden meanings. The jazz was slow, and her voice made any line sound good. More than an hour flew by.

As the entertainment was coming to an end and people were leaving, Gonzalo ran up to our table. "Mister Alain! You must come now! Trouble with the ship!"

Alarmed, Alain apologized to me. "Wait here, Ida. I will be back quickly." Then he and Gonzalo hurried off.

It was sudden and strange. I wondered how he could promise to be back quickly, not knowing the nature of the problem. I was a bit worried as the last song was sung and everyone slowly began to leave. There were still people at many of the tables, and a young boy stepped up on the stage and began to play a guitar. I did not want to walk back to the estate alone, so I decided to sit and stay while there were still people around me.

It grew later and later. Lights were winking out all around me. Most of the patrons had left the restaurant, and Alain had not returned. The young boy still played, but he was taking more breaks. He sat with his father, who was drinking beer at a table between songs.

The restaurant owner came out and let me know that they were closing, but I was welcome to sit outside as long as I liked. I watched the boy and his father. The older man got up unsteadily, hanging his head. The boy got up and pushed him gently. The man held up his head again, and his son proceeded to help him walk down the street, his guitar slung over his back. I watched them slowly disappear into the far darkness of a side alley.

Now the street was empty. I sat alone for a while, nervous, but what came next was truly terrifying. I suddenly noticed a man standing right outside of one of the alleys on my left. The street lamplight shone on him; he was wearing gray and red clothes, and covering his face was a horrific mask, all white with small openings for the eyes and a large red smile painted on it. My body began to shake as he stepped out onto the center of the street, and I saw the long knife in his right hand. He squared his body towards me.

My legs went wobbly, and my heart was pounding so hard against my chest that I could hear it more than anything else. I leaped to my feet and started to run in the opposite direction, but I felt like my legs were rubber, and I could hardly move. I opened my mouth to scream, but no sound came out. I could see his shadow growing closer to me—and then the sound of a shot.

I fell to my knees, gasping. I turned to see what had happened, and the masked man was gone. Luc stood there, holding his revolver. He was gazing into the dark alley.

"I can't believe I missed," he said regretfully. "He saw me before I fired. I don't know how he did...." He then strode over to me and helped me up. Luc gave me a hard look. "Never go out at night without me until this is over. You understand?"

It was still hard for me to speak, but I managed

to squeeze out a "Yes." He then gave me his arm and slowly walked me home without a word. Once in the manor, he made me some sort of drink with orange drops in it, and I drank it. Shortly after, I fell asleep on the couch.

In my dreams, low, slow music played. Clouds came down to ground level, and among them, Eleanor walked through a path in the garden. I felt myself floating above and observing it all. On each side of her in the bushes sat odd creatures. They stared at her with beastly eyes, yet they were also human. Eleanor walked by and then all the way down to the shore. There she stood and watched the waves. In the distance, something large and strange began to rise from the ocean. And then I heard a voice.

CHAPTER SIX

"Wake up, Ida, wake up."

It was Luc. Next to him stood Nigel, looking angry. I opened my eyes and sat up.

"I kept trying to tell him to leave you alone, Lady Ida!" Nigel fumed. "I did! He refused, said you couldn't sleep longer!"

"Yes, Ida, it's not safe to oversleep after the sedative I gave you. Today you can rest, and we can talk about what I have learned. For now, your hysterical butler can see to your breakfast."

Luc smiled and walked off as I calmed Nigel and the dogs, who were also worked up because of the old fellow's nerves. I asked the butler for my usual breakfast. I knew a task would make him feel better, and he left the room, quick to perform his duties

I took a bath and put on fresh clothes. When I came back downstairs, my food was waiting. Nigel pleasantly presented it as always. I thought of calling Luc to join me but then realized I wasn't feeling fully normal yet. Once I picked up my fork to eat the eggs, I couldn't control my hand from shaking. The stress and tension of the frightening event from the night before were still very much with me. I put down the fork and did my best to refocus and take deep breaths. When I tried again, my hands were still shaking, but not as badly. I was able to eat and drink my coffee, and afterwards, I went out and sat in the garden at the small table.

Birds were singing their inspiring and beautiful songs, praising a simple life. The human mind did not allow such simplicity, or did it? Being human, and having moral agency, was a great gift from God, allowing for the greatest good we could do on our planet. But it could also be turned toward the greatest evil.

After I had sat there drinking coffee for about an hour, Luc emerged from the house. He picked up another garden chair and came over to me. "May I sit? Are you feeling more calm?"

"Yes, please. I am...just taking in the beauty here and thinking about how we humans are capable of great good, but also great evil."

Luc folded his arms across his chest. "That doesn't sound like a very relaxing thought, but I would agree that free will is God's greatest gift." He leaned forward onto the table. "So, last night, I found where Guud lives. It's a mansion on the edge of the town, opposite this one, all the way on the other end. It's smaller than yours. The place was dark the whole time I circled around, looking into the windows. I think there is probably something going on in the basement, or maybe he wasn't home. We can go there today and see if we can get a conversation going."

"What about the man in the mask? And what happened to Alain? Oh my God." I closed my eyes and put my hands over my face.

Luc patted my shoulder awkwardly. "He's fine. He came over today very early. He said someone had set his boat on fire. Everyone is uninjured, though. The man in the mask...he's not an ordinary man. He moves very fast, and he's extremely agile. His senses are heightened, and he will prove very elusive. But killers like him won't stop. He will be back. I know the type; I can feel it.

"Today, we will try to talk to Guud, and after, if there is time, we will go down to the fishing village and perhaps speak to that lighthouse keeper you mentioned in your overall assessment — Raul? Maybe he knows something."

I nodded and remained silent for the time being. I leaned back and took a few deep breaths. Things were moving fast, but the faster I could resolve this, the better.

The sky was rather grey, and Nigel insisted I take an umbrella before heading out with Luc. I agreed and was on my way. As we walked the town streets, I felt a little uneasy.

"It's okay feeling nervous around here after your experience. It'll get better. Have you gone to church around here yet, Ida?"

"No, but I was told there are a few, one pretty large and nice. Are you religious?"

"Yes, I'm a Christian. I'll have to visit one of them sometime if you don't mind since it's not work-related."

"I don't. I should probably go sometime myself

as well…and if it helps you feel better, then it is work-related also."

Luc commented, "I try to communicate with God. I'm not sure if it makes me feel better, but it feeds my soul, and sometimes I get answers."

For some reason, this comforted me. "That's wonderful. I'm glad you have that in your life."

We turned away from the main street and into a narrow alley. Compared to the rest of the town, the row houses on this street were rather unkempt and poor-looking. As we passed, here and there, someone would peek through the window to look at us. A few people passed by, almost brushing up against us, as the sidewalk was very narrow.

A child waved at us, sitting on the steps of one of the homes. He looked tired and thin. My heart hurt as I watched him, so I hurried over and gave him a handful of cash. His eyes lit up as he took it and hugged me, filled with gratitude. I turned back to Luc and saw something I had not seen yet in him. His eyes were filled with pride and admiration. He was showing a strong emotional response for the first time since I had met him.

We continued down the street and finally came

out on the other side of the town. This time a wide black road separated us from a medium-height dark rusty fence. Behind it stood an old mansion made out of dark brown stones. The gates were open. There was no garden in the yard, the ground barely had any grass, and all the plants were dead, with the exception of the weeds. There was one large twisted, dead tree on the right side. We came up to a door, which once was probably a perfect blue color, but now only had a hint of it left. Luc knocked. He had to repeat the motion several times before we finally heard a distant voice from the inside and waited.

The door opened, and there stood a man in a white coat and black pants, of medium height and stocky. He had a large head, a balding scalp, and a wrinkled forehead. His dark eyes stared at us with a calm gaze.

"Yes?"

"Mr. Guud?"

"That's correct. You?"

"This is Ida Clifton. I am Investigator Luc Nistage."

The wrinkled brow lifted. "Huh. A Clifton, yes, so that's how you look. And an investigator. Well, come in. I could use a break for some entertainment."

Luc and I exchanged a look as we crossed the threshold. The inside of the house was dim and dark. Guud lit a candle in one of the rooms and pointed for us to sit on an old black couch. He sat across from us and lit a cigarette. I could see Luc grimace slightly. He evidently shared my dislike for the habit.

"So, Luc, you working for the government? Special investigator for the island?"

"No, I'm a private eye."

Guud blew smoke toward the ceiling. "Oh, an individual investigator, not connected with any big establishments. Great, I respect that. There is no one I loathe more than mindless minions who do their masters' bidding without questioning anything."

There was a pause before Luc answered. "What if those minions were to serve you?"

The man shrugged. "I'd loathe them even more. Useful idiots will get no respect from me."

"Hmm. Well, Mr. Guud—"

"Doctor, please."

"Dr. Guud, you are a well-known man around here from what I learned. I hoped by coming here I could gain some valuable information."

"About?"

"The island, perhaps the Blackswans. The murders, disappearances. You've lived here your whole life, no?"

Dr. Guud stubbed out his cigarette in an ashtray. "No. Almost my whole life. I studied in Germany under a young talented genius, Dr. Schmitt. Then I came back here to find myself, my own practice. But something was missing. A long time passed, and later I went back to Germany for a few years. In the 1930s, I met a young man, much younger than I but so much greater. His name was Mengele. I learned more from him in those few years than in all the years before combined. I came back here again, and that is when my research improved tremendously."

"I've read that you helped a lot of people. Is that the focus of your research, to improve life?"

Guud snorted. "Oh, haha. What does it mean 'to improve life'? Men cling to...," he waved his hand in the air, "some moral codes. They create dreams in their heads. I don't know what 'a better life' means."

Luc regarded him appraisingly. "You don't have a moral code?"

"Of course not. The only thing that exists for

me is discovery, and things that stand in the way of, or things that aid it."

"Do you know much about the Blackswans?" Luc changed the subject, but I would have liked to hear more about the doctor's personal philosophies.

He lit another cigarette. "Old rich family, disappeared? Agakon, perhaps? If you believe such things."

"Agakon?"

"Oh boy. I see I've hit on something neither of you knows. No surprise, honestly — many who live here their entire lives are clueless too. Agakon is a cult, mostly operating in the Burg region, though there are some in Everette. They worship a large fish, some sea creature. They think he takes people into the sea and makes them...," here he wiggled his fingers in air quotes, "'powerful.' They all want him to take them, I guess. Why not? Maybe it's true. Humph." Guud puffed on the cigarette.

Luc had a thoughtful look on his face. "That's a fascinating theory. I see I have to deepen my research."

"Be careful."

"What about the other issue?"

"The murders, attacks?"

"Yes."

Guud shrugged, stubbing out his cigarette again. "Absolutely no clue."

We cordially parted ways with him. Once we were clear from the house, however, I saw a change in Luc's face.

"He was very eager to tell us about the cult," Luc mused, almost too quietly for me to hear him. "His tone about the Blackswans was clearly resentful, and the way he spoke to you indicates perhaps he did not like the Cliftons as well. The one issue he was quick to dismiss was the murders, but he also spoke of attacks. I said nothing of that to him. What attacks? We must investigate more. He clearly knows something about it. I'll have to keep an eye on his place."

"What do you mean by 'keeping an eye?'" I asked warily.

"I'll hide and watch for the whole night."

I squared my shoulders and said resolutely, "I will do it with you."

Luc glanced at me sideways. "Huh...sure. We will see if you can last."

My eyes narrowed at him. "Don't underestimate me."

"We'll see…now we go back. Actually, after we rest, how about dinner in town, and I promise you'll be safe." He smiled. "I understand there is a jazz singer?"

"Yes, I heard her last night."

Luc nodded. "Great, we can do that tonight, and tomorrow we can visit the other regions and stake out Guud's mansion."

We walked back home. I thought of Alain. He must have felt badly about what happened. I wondered if he was going to the café again tonight. He might get the idea that Luc and I were out together on a date. I sighed.

Luc looked at me sideways and smiled. "I know it's hard, but do your best to enjoy the moments that are good and don't fill them with bad thoughts. You will rob yourself of present joys by doing that. Trust me—I know all too well."

His voice was calm, and the kindness of his words touched me. I remembered him telling me that he had spent several years in prison due to a setup. I wanted to ask him about it, but I could not figure out how to bring up such a delicate subject that was undoubtedly a source of pain.

When we got back, Nigel greeted us with excitement. He showed me a large bouquet of flowers in the main sitting room and said Alain had brought them for me. Luc made no comment.

We ate and went to separate parts of the house to wait for evening. Luc went into his room, saying he'd work on his notes and read more about the Blackswans. I went to the balcony on the top floor and, with tea in hand, watched the slow sunset over the calm, magnificent ocean.

As I enjoyed the scenery, I had the feeling of someone watching me from far away, just as I had before. It was a strange and inexplicable thing. I just wanted to calmly relax and enjoy the end of the sun's beautiful workday, but even this did not seem fully possible. Would Luc be able to solve these mysteries, and after that, would I feel calm and safe? Perhaps it was unwise to have put so much faith in one person, especially one who had a troubled past.

After the sunset, I got a blanket to ward off the evening chill as I stayed on the balcony to watch the moon and stars begin to appear. I must have drifted off again. I saw myself standing on the edge of the cliffs, a thin mist around me, and the waves violently smashing against the rocks below. I heard someone behind me and turned around. There was someone coming out of the mist holding what looked like a knife, but then a strong breeze blew.

I woke up and realized I was on the balcony with my blanket on the floor. Then I heard Luc's voice inside the house calling for me. He was ready to get going. I must have been asleep longer than I realized.

The night was slightly chillier than usual due to a stronger breeze. I walked close to Luc, and he realized that the breeze was coming from the left; he stepped around me to walk on that side. I smiled to myself as he did this in a funny way, pretending he saw something in a bush on the left first as if he did not want the credit for being a gentleman. The main street was nicely lit as we walked by La Dame Ava and turned into the following street to find the same eatery I had been at the night before. As before, people were already gathering, and we took a table farther from the stage, close to the brick wall of one of the townhomes. The boy with the guitar was back, and his father looked like he had already begun drinking heavily. We ordered some food and lemonades, but Luc avoided alcohol, so I decided not to imbibe either.

Finally, the band was ready, and wonderful Emmanuela walked onto the stage and began her second performance of the month, and apparently the last one of the year.

"And the ship has sailed away
And the waves hugged it tightly
As the beacon of a lighthouse
Shone oh so brightly...

Oh my love
with this light
guide me
Oh my love
in this night
don't fight me.

Sunset of sorrow
Winds of tomorrow
Gleam of hope

in the eyes
of the storm.

Oh my love,
Oh my love,
In this storm
you guide me.
Oh my love,
Oh my love,
In your arms
you invite me.

A sunrise together
A sunrise of faith
Forever and ever
Growing old
In loving ways."

The song went on and on, long, slow, and beautiful. I looked over at Luc. He was watching the stage, but in his eyes, I saw nostalgia and a hint of sadness. He was hearing the music and was absorbed in it, but at the same time, he seemed to be looking past the performer as if he were lost in a vision from the past.

When the music stopped, and there was a break, I finally had the courage to ask. "Why this look in your eyes?"

Luc came back to the present and looked me in the eyes. "This takes me back…to another Paradise."

Intrigued, I asked, "What really happened to you?"

"I fell in love with a woman. Then I killed her."

I felt my eyes get large, and my jaw drop. He laughed.

"That's a very simplified version…."

Before I could think, I replied, "Well, don't fall in love with me, then!"

I wasn't sure what to make of this conversation as another song began. Luc's offhand answer was at the same time funny, frightening, and annoyingly incomplete. Certainly, this enigmatic man had not committed cold-blooded murder. What did he really mean? Perhaps his answer was designed to make sure I did not ask again. I was burning with curiosity, but I decided not to pursue the question. I just sat there listening to the music the rest of the evening.

When the band stopped for the night, I again

worried that Alain might have seen me and gotten the wrong idea. I made a mental note to seek him out in the morning.

Luc and I slowly strolled along the nighttime streets as we made our way back to the mansion. As we passed a dark alley, Luc glanced into it.

"It seems to be a peaceful night, yet there is a possibility that in one of the streets in this town, the killer is lurking, looking for his next victim." He stopped speaking, lost in thought for a few moments. "You know…I think we should stick to our plan of visiting other regions tomorrow, but the following night, we must stake out Guud's house. We need to work hard. We don't want the victim count to go up."

I agreed, feeling a bit tired. I was looking forward to getting into my bed and getting some restful sleep.

However, as I was preparing for bed in my room, again, I had the feeling that someone was watching me. I glanced sideways at Eleanor's portrait, and the canvas was blank! I turned to look at it squarely, and no, it was still there, Eleanor as beautiful as ever, looking right back at me. I took a deep breath and sighed. I must really be allowing my fatigue and fear to get the better of me.

Once changed, I got into bed with a candle, and after a few minutes, I put it out. I could hear the dogs outside my door, lying against it. I thought I was brave enough to sleep on my own but was I really? A twinge of fear tugged at my mind. It took me a long time to relax and drift away.

Suddenly I stood deep in the ocean on a dark road made from black stones. I could breathe underwater and slowly began to walk on the road, which seemed to lead toward a large, dark structure in the distance.

With caution, I entered what seemed to be an ancient city. Each wall and dark building had engravings. From the deep dark center of the city, I heard a voice, but it wasn't human, and it spoke in a language I could not understand. I was terrified, but I continued to move forward. Something was drawing me in.

"No, not there. Not like them, not you!"

I heard a female voice behind me and felt a hand on my shoulder. I turned and stood face to face with Eleanor. Her eyes were filled with grief as she embraced me.

I woke up.

It was already morning. I could smell coffee brewing on the first floor. The delicious scent rousted me out of bed and made me get ready faster than usual.

CHAPTER SEVEN

Downstairs Luc was sitting at the dining table. Breakfast was ready, with coffee and tea. Luc motioned towards it.

"After we eat, we will set off for our very busy day of exploration with no car since there aren't any on this island," he said wryly.

I realized that he had just found out about the lack of cars from Nigel and laughed at the incredulous look on his face.

Luc didn't laugh, but his eyes held a hint of amusement. "Yes, it's funny, how many years ago towns and cities already were filled with them, yet here we are on Paradise Shores, where there are no cars allowed! Something about 'mother nature' or what? You think these 'paradise' places can't get crazier, but they always do."

He shook his head and sipped some more coffee. I joined him, still smiling at his reaction.

Suddenly Mark rushed in, looking panicked. Nigel followed him right behind and hurried up to us. "Lady Ida, Mr. Luc, there has been another victim found, a young lady."

Luc got up and put on his coat immediately. "We must go now. I must see the body. Come with me, Ida. You have clout in this town in case they are reluctant to trust me."

"Can you ride?" I asked Luc.

He grimaced. "I can if I have to, and this time I think I have to."

Mark hurried to saddle some horses for us, and we galloped off to the police station.

I still had not met Chief Clum or Sheriff Lindon, but I did remember what Mayor Konig had told me about them. I told Luc that, according to the mayor, they were stubborn and not particularly bright.

He snorted. "That's not unusual," he said.

I thought about how strange and sad it was that Luc was spot on last night when he spoke about the killer possibly stalking someone. We rushed through the streets as fast as we could. I wanted to make sure Luc could see the body as quickly as possible.

The police station was tiny. As we entered, we were greeted by a man with a stern face, in his fifties, with short grey hair. He introduced himself as Sheriff Lindon. I was relieved and surprised that, after only a short discussion, he gave us permission to see the body, which had been transferred to the morgue, located in the Everett region by the cliffs. We took the paper and thanked him. We planned to go to those parts anyway, so it wasn't that big of an inconvenience.

We decided to take the carriage and headed back to the mansion. Mark harnessed fresh horses, and we were swiftly on our way. The weather was clear, and the fields looked beautiful as we felt a very light breeze coming up from the ocean.

Luc sighed. "Perfect weather, but what an unfortunate event. Such is the nature of this line of work." He shook his head and changed the subject. "You said you met Raul down there?"

Luc pointed to the right as the farm, and giant lighthouse were in our sights.

"Yes. He is a rather strange fellow, but from what I've been told, very capable."

"Who told you this?"

"Alain."

Luc raised his brows. "I'll have to speak to this Raul also at some point."

We got to the tall cliffs, and there behind a long, fenced area, stood the morgue. As we got out of the carriage and walked up to the old grey building, there was not a person in sight. The breeze up there was stronger.

The doors were old, a worn and faded red. We entered. The first floor was almost empty. There was a desk in the back with a middle-aged lady sitting behind it. She glanced at us and waved us over. She had a name tag stating, "Sue."

"We are here to see the latest victim." Luc got right to the point and handed Sue the paper from Lindon.

She looked it over silently, then stood and motioned for us to follow her. We entered a dark room. There was a strong stench, and on a metal table lay the body of the girl. I felt sick, and suddenly I was unable to breathe. Luc grabbed me by the shoulder as he saw I was about to collapse and led me out. I sat on a bench, trying to calm myself and breathe normally, while he went in alone. It took me some time to calm down, and by the time I felt better, Luc had come out. We thanked Sue and went outside.

"I know these things are tough to see and hear, but you wanted to do this, Ida. Are you okay? Do you want to talk about it?"

I nodded quickly. "Yes, please."

Luc looked away, then at me again. "This girl was killed by a curved knife. The marks are very different from the body I examined previously. The other victim was a man with no family. He is scheduled to be cremated soon. All the other victims have been buried or cremated at this point. From the reports I read, most of the victims were young females, but there were other victims of all ages and both sexes. This leads me to believe that we possibly have two killers. One is being covered by the other's killings."

I was stunned. "Do you think they are working together?"

Luc shook his head. "No, I don't think so. I believe one is perhaps a very compulsive predator, uncontrollable, who kills anyone he can find. The other is more careful and specific, and he kills only young women."

"This makes matters more complicated if true."

"Yes, it does," Luc said, shaking his head again. "But we will get them. Let's head to Burg now."

I was still shaken about the dead body. Feelings of sadness and compassion for the poor girl overcame me, but also a sense of horror and dread. What had she felt in her final moments? Total and complete despair? This wasn't a peaceful passing from old age. How twisted was the person who could do such a thing?

"There are many evil people in the world, but also many good and wonderful people," Luc said this as if reading my mind.

I looked at him as the carriage lurched along. "I know," I said, turning my head to look out the window. It was all I could muster. I was unable to put my thoughts into words without letting emotions take over.

"What worries us, sometimes overcomes us, sometimes helps us grow stronger and forge a new path and a stronger identity." Luc paused and looked out into the green fields we were passing, his eyes narrow and becoming nostalgic again. "When I was in my twenties, I went through the hardest trial of my life, but I also met a man who led me closer to God. My faith has helped me to stay strong."

We entered the forest region now and were heading down the road leading directly into the Burg village. When we arrived, I was quite surprised to see how large this village was, spread out far and wide.

Mark tied the horses near a pub. I turned to Luc with a questioning look. He pointed at the message board in front of the pub. It had various announcements and village news tacked to it. Luc stood in front of it, carefully poring over every scrap of information. "There." He pointed at one news posting. "'Attack on Abigail Smith.'"

The item said the victim had survived and was now at home, but it was still unknown who or what had attacked her. It also said hers was the ninth such attack in recent times.

"That is very strange," Luc mused. "We must speak to Abigail and, I hope, a few of the other victims."

Luc approached one of the locals, a young lad. At first, the boy looked wary and did not want to talk to us, but when Luc took out a few dollars, not only did the boy talk, but he told us where several of the victims lived, including Abigail.

We decided to walk through the village towards Abigail's house, which was, according to the boy, at the end of the northern part of the village. Almost everyone turned to stare at us. Most people gave us looks of frustration and displeasure. Only the kids didn't seem to care much.

Luc smiled. "They really seem to love us," he muttered to me. I appreciated his humor, but I was also nervous. He noticed and smiled again. "These people are safe, safer than those in the town. Ida, remember, fake smiles, fake laughter, it's fake goodness. None of that matters when disasters come. You remember the story of the Good Samaritan? It's like that. These simple folk are the ones that more likely would help you if an extreme situation came up."

I had to admit that he was right. His words did calm me, but of course, there were exceptions on both sides.

We came upon a small house, grey with age. Luc knocked on the door, and a short old lady with grey hair and a concerned look opened the door. Luc asked about Abigail, and the lady invited us inside. She then went to fetch her granddaughter, and we both sat on a wooden bench.

A young woman came into the room with a large dark bruise on the right side of her face. She was limping and had bandages around her left hand and midsection. Abigail's eyes were sad as she sat not far from us on a simple old wooden chair. My heart surged with compassion for this poor girl.

"Who are you?"

"Hello, Abigail. This is Ida Clifton, and I am Luc Nistage, private investigator."

Suddenly I realized that the first thing that should be done was to reach out in kindness. "Abigail, have you been taken care of properly?" I asked, looking the girl in the eyes. "I'd like to give you some money to help you and your family."

I took out a decent amount of cash from my purse and handed it to her. She accepted reluctantly and timidly but with great gratitude. She managed a weak smile. "I will tell you all I can."

Luc's face was impassive, but not to me. I could see the excitement in his eyes. He proceeded to ask her some questions. "Abigail, first, tell me in detail what you were doing before the attack and where it occurred."

The girl sighed and began. "It was a sunny day. I went to pick wild mushrooms, as I often did — do. We make soup, which lasts us a while. I usually have to go deep inside the forest, closer to the tall hills, but sometimes I head towards the ocean. The forest goes almost all the way to the water on that side. I went towards the hill that day. I was about halfway, near a small creek and a waterfall we have there. It's the only one. That's when it happened."

"Can you describe your attacker?" Luc asked gently.

"It happened fast…it was on top of me in an instant, formed like a man, I think, but with fur and claws." Tears formed in Abigail's eyes. "I'm not sure. But he was trying to kill me! I was in absolute terror, fighting to get away. Then I think he attacked something else. I think I heard a fox screaming, but I did not look at anything. I just ran. Despite my injuries and bleeding, I ran faster than ever before. I heard that animal, or whatever it was, behind me again, but I got inside the village just in time, and people saw me and ran to help me." The girl squeezed her eyes shut as tears ran down her face.

I reached out and held her hand.

"Thank you, Abigail. I am so sorry," Luc said. "Could you draw us a map of the area? Then we will be off."

Abigail drew us a primitive map and thanked us for the money again. We went on our way to seek out the other victims.

Astonishingly, John Doodin, Janet Kin, and Mike Lum all had similar stories, with one huge exception: Each described the creature differently and had been attacked in different places, but all of them did agree it resembled a human.

The day began to wane, and Luc suggested that we go back and implement our night plan to stake out Guud's mansion and save for another day our trip into the Burg forest. I agreed, and Mark took us back just as the sun was setting. Luc said he would rest before going out. I decided to first watch the sunset on the balcony and then take a nap.

This time I was very aware of myself and had

no tremendous fatigue. I stayed awake throughout the beautiful scene and then lay down on my bed. As I slowly closed my eyes to nap, I saw Eleanor's face appear to me in the darkness. Then there was nothing, and in this nothingness, small white light particles began to float all around me. I watched them with astonishment. Were they just part of this dream?

CHAPTER EIGHT

A few hours later, when I woke up, I still remembered those particles floating around me. I tried to look into the space in front of me and see something I couldn't perceive before, but alas, there was nothing. Perhaps it came when the brain was in a more relaxed mode.

I got up and got dressed appropriately for the night outing in dark, well-fitting clothes. Right outside my door lay the dogs, who were very calm and relaxed as they looked up at me with their big brown eyes.

"Hello, my beauties."

I squatted down to scratch them behind the ears, and they looked like they'd just entered heaven.

A moment later, they stood up and looked down the stairs. I looked also and saw Luc walk by the stairs holding a book. He looked up and noticed us, but all he did was wave and calmly walk into the sitting room. The dogs slowly walked down the steps by my side. I followed Luc into the room and found him sitting there by the fire. He gazed into the flames, lost in thought, with the closed book in his hands. I sat in a soft chair across from him. The dogs lay between us on the carpet. The logs crackled. We sat in silence until he slowly turned his head to me. His eyes seemed to have come back into this reality.

"I finished reading about the Blackswans."

"And?"

Luc shook his head. "They were a very troubled family. Although this book was careful not to go into specifics, I am sure almost all were members of the Agakon cult. Except for Mary and Eleanor, and perhaps Theodore, who may even be alive still."

"But how is that possible?" I interrupted, astonished. "They disappeared nearly eighty years ago!"

"There is a mention of a seer, a wise man who lived in the forest. He had a son he was raising and teaching all he knew. The son's name was Ognog. Apparently, Theodore knew Ognog. There is a description of where Ognog lived. Perhaps we can locate the place."

"You think this Ognog if we can find him, will tell us something important?"

Luc nodded solemnly. "Perhaps whether Theodore is still alive, and maybe something about this cult." He stood up. "Anyway, we will be going to stake out Guud's house soon. Are you sure you're up for it?"

"Yes," I answered with resolve and confidence. I hoped this would leave Luc without doubts. I had to be part of this.

CHAPTER NINE

The air that night was thin, and it was colder than usual. Luc led me through the streets along the back side of the town. "It will be better if no one sees us," he said, and though it took longer to go around that way, I trusted his experience in these matters.

We passed through a street filled with potholes and dark puddles. On the sidewalks, up against buildings, lay people wrapped in coats and blankets, sleeping. I was shocked to see such a thing, but there was no time to dwell on their misfortune as Luc motioned me to keep going.

Just around the corner, above a crooked and dim streetlamp, was a window with peeling paint and cracked panes. An old man with a wrinkled face leaned out of it, smoking, his eyes fixed on one of the puddles below. He did not seem to notice us.

We headed into a grove of trees and bushes. It gave into the forest on the right, but to the left was Guud's mansion.

The wind picked up from time to time, but mostly it was calm and quiet. There were still plenty of lights in the town, as people had tried to brighten the streets at night due to the recent events. I leaned back against a tree trunk, surrounded by bushes. Luc was on his knees, looking through an opening between them.

An hour had passed, and the only thing I heard was an owl, which wasn't too far from us in one of the trees. Luc still remained in the same position.

"Aren't you tired of not moving at all?" I whispered.

"We have just begun. I'm used to this, not tired in the slightest. You can relax more if you'd like, and I'll alert you if I see anything."

I frowned into the darkness. "I feel like that wouldn't be the right way to contribute."

"Nonsense. You are already doing a lot. Don't tire yourself out. Your mind will start to wander too much."

"If you say so."

I leaned back more and made a pillow of my scarf, which I put behind my head. I closed my eyes and tried my best to relax, listening to the forest. It must have worked since, after some time, I felt Luc shaking my arm. I slowly opened my eyes. He signaled for me to be quiet and pointed at something through the opening in the bushes. What I saw next chilled me to the bones, and a sense of strange terror overcame me.

Out of the forest came a creature, neither human nor beast. It seemed to be a mix of both. It walked on all fours, but the front legs were very hairy and more like furry arms with sharp claws on the tips of the fingers. The back legs resembled those of a goat. The face was most disturbing. It was droopy and dull with fur on the sides of the cheeks, large pitch-black eyes, and no hair on its head, just a small horn in the center of the skull. Its back was covered with fur. The overall size was that of a large man.

As we watched in horrified fascination, the creature made a sound which was unlike anything I had ever heard. It moved towards the mansion, and once it was next to the wall, a secret door leading down into the cellar opened up. Once the creature was fully inside, the door closed. It was quiet again. I heard Luc swallow, and I could also hear my heart pounding very clearly, and my hands were shaking.

Luc slowly turned his head to face me. "I think that's enough for you for tonight. Let's get back into town quietly."

He helped me up and kept looking around, alert to any sounds or movements. I could barely walk straight and had to lean on him. He was clearly nervous, as he obviously did not want us to run into another one of those creatures. Luckily we got to the town streets safely and slowly continued all the way home. Once inside the house and in the sitting room, Luc once again gave me his sleeping mixture and, this time, helped me to my bed. I fell right to sleep in spite of the fear, thanks to the potion.

Empty — the dream was mostly empty. Darkness. Except for a pair of eyes appearing from time to time. These eyes knew me — or perhaps they were my own eyes, watching my body? Was it my spirit? This strange condition continued until I woke up.

I actually felt fresh and strong but mentally still struck by what I had seen. It was late morning, and after I got ready for the day, I was informed by Nigel that Alain was waiting at the little table outside in the garden. I hurried to greet him. We embraced, and I sat with him as Nigel brought us coffee and breakfast.

"I'm so sorry I didn't put in more effort to see you recently. I was gone from the island for several days. I have a new ship now! I'll have to watch it more carefully. Someone really doesn't like me in this town." He shrugged helplessly. "I don't know why. Have you gotten used to this island life yet? It's too bad you had to get here during such a terrible time. I felt so bad for leaving you that night and finding out that you were in danger." He grasped my hand. "Are you all right?"

"I understand, and I'm glad you are okay. I am just fine, so that's behind us." I sipped my coffee and bit into a fresh, flaky croissant. "Do you have any idea who could have set your boat on fire?"

"No. Not a clue. There have been rumors of an old cult being active in the forests and at sea, but I'm not sure there would be a connection."

"Yes, I've heard of it…we are investigating." I took another bite of the croissant.

Alain appeared to be only mildly interested. "He's a good detective? Are you pleased?"

"Very, he's been very helpful and knowledgeable."

"That's good! So you have plans today?"

"I actually have to find out from Luc. We might have to investigate something together, although we had quite a late night."

"Well, don't push yourself too hard then. When the mind is clear, you can do twice as much good work in half the time." Alain smiled at me indulgently.

"Perhaps you're right. I ought to let Luc go alone this time."

Indeed, after Alain left, I made the decision to rest and take some time out, so the investigator set off on his own.

At this point in my story, I would like to share what happened straight from Luc's own personal record about this case, which was given to me at a later date:

Paradise Shores investigation entry number 11. Luc Nistage.

This island did not weigh heavy on me yet — nevertheless, I couldn't help but feel a similarity to that dreadful case so many years ago.

Ida told me to go out alone this day, and frankly, I was very relieved. She looked pale and drained, and I had a feeling deep inside that this outing would be a dangerous one.

I took a single horse with me and asked Mark to stay home, a move I'm sure he appreciated. I set off to examine the locations of the attacks in the forests, although now I could imagine what the creatures were after seeing one the night before.

They had to be the results of Guud's genetic experiments. Another twisted scientist doctor to contend with — what a pleasure.

Wind blew strongly into my face as I rode through the vast fields and hills. In the distance, I saw the large lighthouse, which unlike a previous one I remembered well, filled me with dread instead of peace. The forests and the village seemed to be much closer together this time, as I was traveling alone and making better time.

When I arrived at the village, I saw a few men from

town cutting down some trees near the outskirts. I tied the horse to a tree and headed into the forest, following the directions the young girl gave us.

There was the fresh smell of green leaves and a mossy sort of atmosphere, very dank, a bit strange for these parts. I moved slowly as I looked around often and carefully, listening to every sound. There was no room for mistakes in this game.

I saw many insects I had never seen on the mainland. I must admit that only then did I realize my senses were more heightened without Ida around. I was too focused on her safety rather than general observation when she was with me. I had learned to do this alone. The only time someone had teamed up with me before this was an experience I can never forget.

Finally, I reached a formation of stones against a hill. Bushes and trees were all around me. I sat down, watching my surroundings carefully. There was nothing I could see that gave me any insights, but this was the spot where young Abigail had been assaulted.

There were other spots to investigate given to us by a few victims besides the young woman. I headed back to where I had left my horse. I was slow, for I had to be constantly alert, and this was burning up precious time *before the dark came, but it had to be done this way.*

The woodsmen were gone, and the horse looked at me with sad eyes. From the bag I had strapped onto him, I took out an apple and fed him while petting him. What a good animal. Then I strapped on his feed bag.

"I'll be back soon."

With those words, I ventured into the other side of the forest, towards the ocean. The colors of the sky were already starting to change to a slightly purple-pink color. As I continued through the forest, I felt the ocean breeze, so familiar this time. I could feel past memories flooding into my mind, but I did my best to ignore them, as I had to stay focused on my surroundings. What came next should not have shaken me, for I had experience, but it still did.

In the distance, I began to hear the sound of low rhythmic drumming and chanting. My heart began to beat faster as I continued through the thick bushes and trees, getting closer to the sounds. As I reached the source, I had to duck down quickly and hide.

In the open field before me stood many people dressed in black robes. They formed a large circle and chanted. On the side stood two who were hitting the drums with their hands. They held their arms up into the air, but every time the chants stopped, they lowered them. They continued the chants on and off until it began to get dark. Then they lit torches, and out of the bushes, others dressed in robes brought out three people, two men and one woman, who were bound. Their hands were in chains, and they each had a chain around their neck, and it looked as though their mouths were sewn shut. Chills ran down my spine. This was a sacrifice to the fish demon they worshipped! The cult members formed a procession and began to march towards the ocean. I carefully followed, staying out of sight in the bushes. Finally, we reached the cliffs. I was frozen in place as the cultists lined up along the cliffs and hung the three victims from the rocks by their ankles.

One of them took off his hood and revealed his strong face with a big blond beard and messy hair. "I, Lief, the high priest, call upon you! Agakon, accept these gifts and bless us once again with power!"

Everyone else began to chant the creature's name. "Agakon! Agakon! Agakon!"

As they chanted, I felt and heard the bushes move near me. I made no sudden movements and ever so slightly looked to my right side. One of Guud's deformed creatures sat there. I looked to my left, and another one of them hid in the undergrowth there. My blood chilled as I did my best to focus on breathing as quietly as possible. I dearly hoped they could not smell me. These beasts must have come here to grab one or two of the cultists if any were separated in the forest in the dark. Some of the victims must have lied...some were cultists...are cultists. Was the entire village involved? I was shocked at how I had made such a grave miscalculation and misjudged the situation on this island.

I brought my mind to the present as I heard and saw the water below the cliffs violently swirl and move. The true horror came next. A giant creature with the huge head of a fish, many big black eyes, an enormous mouth filled with rows of teeth, and four massive arms, emerged out of the water. It climbed part way up the rocks and then stopped. Agakon looked up at the dangling victims and, with one incredibly powerful and fast leap upwards, grabbed all three with his mouth. Just like that, he was gone into the ocean. The chains were dangling – there with no remains. I was giddy with true terror, as I had not felt for years since my last encounter with a similar creature.

I sat silently in the bush. As the cultists went back into the forest, so did the creatures, surely to try and snatch a few for themselves.

I remained there for at least an hour to make sure it was safe to come out. Eventually, I made it back to the spot, but sadly the ropes from my horse were just hanging there. Either the creatures or the cultists had taken him. I began my long walk back to the mansion.

As I came out of the forest and was about to head towards the fields and the hills, I thought I saw a faint light among the trees far down to the left, on the ocean side. It wasn't near the village, nor was it near the lighthouse. I crept through the trees and found a small house with a fireplace illuminating the window. I looked inside. It was a one room tiny home with a wooden bed and a pot near the fire, but I saw no one inside. Then I was utterly startled when I heard an old voice behind me. I turned around and pointed my revolver at an old man.

"I reckon you are not really lost, not in the woods at least, but maybe some other way."

He was calm in the face of the revolver. I slowly lowered it but said nothing yet.

"You came here to look, which means you were curious. Now you are silent? Do you want to come in and ask something?"

I nodded as he opened the door. I sat in the corner as he sat near the pot on the fire.

"Mushroom soup. So, who are you?" he asked as he stirred.

"Luc Nistage, private investigator."

"Hah…I asked who are YOU. Isn't that interesting. We say a name and profession, but that is not who you are, is it? What makes you…you?"

"Many things."

"What is your meaning, your goal?"

"To solve riddles."

"To help people, or for redemption? I can tell by your eyes it's not for money."

"Both."

"Hmmm…."

"Are you Ognog?"

"Ah, now, that is good investigating, sort of. I am a man who found meaning in living with nature, thinking about God, about the stars. Sometimes I am a man who dreams of a family, one I used to have."

"You are Theodore Blackswan, aren't you?"

The man became silent for several minutes. As he watched the fire, his eyes became sad. "Yes," he finally said.

"Can you help me with — ?"

He raised his hand, interrupting me. "To help you with the mystery of my family. The answer is there, in the house. The woman who is there now. The answer is with her."

"I don't understand."

"You are smart. You think about it when you get back there."

"What about the cult?"

"What about them? Do you intend to save the world from all evils?"

"But they must be stopped."

"Evil will always exist, much evil and much good. If you try to battle evil on many fronts, you will end up accomplishing nothing on any front. Ah, I see you have a slight smile. You have had a different experience, I see. In your past, you went through pain but accomplished much."

"My task here is to help Ida. You are right. That's the main task."

"So think about it. Think of what I told you when you get back to the mansion."

I was confused but agreed, and after a good helping of delicious mushroom soup, I left.

Entry 11 complete.

At this point, I, Ida Clifton, will pick again and share what happened when Luc came back to the mansion.

I stayed up all night as worry and fear for Luc began to grip my spirit, and I was weak with relief when he returned. Exhausted and worn out, instead of resting, he asked me to sit in a chair near the fireplace. He got all of my documents and his and dumped them on the table in front of us. He sat there looking through them frantically, from time to time stopping and looking at me. "The answer...the answer...."

And then suddenly, he froze, and his eyes got big as he pulled out what looked like my grandmother's birth certificate. "Of course...it was so obvious...how could I have missed it?"

"What? What is it?" I asked, half in fear.

"Your grandmother was born on the mainland a year after Mary escaped the island. No wonder you look so much like Eleanor."

My mouth dropped open in astonishment. "What are you saying? And I don't look like her at all."

He stood up straight and looked at me, bemused. "How could you not notice it?"

He left me there for a moment. He ran to

another room and brought out a long mirror. Then he ran up the stairs and brought down the portrait of Eleanor.

"Look!"

Perhaps before this, my mind had been closed to it, but as I stood looking at my reflection next to the portrait, I saw nearly an identical person. I shook my head and sat back into the chair.

"You are a Blackswan, Ida. Your grandmother was a Blackswan. That's why she came to this island and lived here. That was the secret for you to uncover. Perhaps Eleanor, whom I assume is buried somewhere here, has been trying to connect with you."

I remained silent, looking down at my hands in my lap. "I have some things to tell you." And I related the strange experiences with the portrait, the dreams, the times I thought I had seen Eleanor, and the feeling of being watched.

Luc sat back into the chair and threw his head back, sighing. "Two mysteries solved, the hardest one still left to go."

I glanced up at him, trying not to show my confusion and shock and a bit ashamed at my refusal to see the resemblance.

He noticed my glance. "You did nothing wrong, Ida. You did very well, in fact. You've had so much to deal with. You are a strong person."

We sat in silence for a while. I tried to straighten my thoughts, to collect them. Eventually, Luc went to his room and suggested I go rest, as it was already daylight and neither of us had slept. I let Nigel know that I'd be having a very late breakfast as I slowly went up to my room and collapsed onto the bed.

I woke up around one. The sun was shining brightly through the window. I still felt tired as I rolled over and tried to hide my face from the light. My mind instantly went to the painting, and I looked at the wall but then remembered that it was still downstairs.

Was I supposed to communicate with her? I sat up in bed, wondering. I had learned about my family roots in the strangest way, but I had to be grateful for the revelation.

I walked into the bathroom and looked at my reflection. Yes, absolutely, it was so obvious now. Perhaps my denial had arisen from my strange and frightening experiences with the painting. Was

Eleanor really here? I felt now that she meant me no harm.

I heard a knock on the door.

"Everything okay?"

It was Luc. I replied that I was going to be down to eat shortly. I could hear the dogs breathing heavily by the door. They must have just come in from a run.

I dressed quickly, to find Luc was waiting by the staircase. "Let's go out to eat and perhaps have a conversation which won't raise our heart rates too much, for once."

I laughed and agreed. He wanted to try La Dame Ava Café and Bakery, and I surely did not mind going back to that lovely and cozy place.

Tomas was there, but only he alone. He told us his wife and son were out buying groceries from the village. I saw Luc's face tense up a little bit. He hadn't yet told me about his trip alone. I wondered what he had seen, but we did agree to try and have a conversation on the calmer side. We ordered eggs with strawberries and coffee. Luc got bacon on a separate plate, and I was tempted by a pear pastry.

We sat down by the window. The day outside was truly lovely. I could tell Luc was doing his best to relax his face.

Outside, right by the stone-paved road, were three children playing. They were throwing dice and laughing — two boys and one girl. They resembled each other, so they must have been siblings.

"Such pure joy…a golden age."

"Golden if the child has good parents, present parents."

"Yes, most certainly."

Our coffee and food came. I slowly sipped some of my hot coffee and took a bite of the delicious pastry. I looked at Luc, but he was still watching the kids outside. His gaze seemed to have transformed into a mix of joyful memories but, at the same time, nostalgic.

"Before my first big case, even after I was no longer a child…even then, life was so simple compared to what I learned later." He turned to his food. He sipped the coffee and looked at me. "But moments like these are joyful also, don't you think?"

"Oh yes, of course!" I thought about his habit of making tea every evening. "I've seen you make black tea every night. Many people say it keeps one awake. Is that why?"

Luc set down his cup. "It actually calms me down. Funny, isn't it? It makes my mind function better, slows down the flow of thoughts and sorts them, helps me reason more clearly."

"I know we weren't supposed to talk about intense experiences, but I'm dying to know what happened when you went to the village."

Luc's face became slightly grim as he leaned back in his chair. His head lowered slightly. "It was a horror that I wish you didn't have to know, but you are part of it now."

He paused for a while and finished his coffee. Then he went up to the counter and got refills for both of us.

"When I had the case that changed my life, all those years ago, I learned of many mysteries. Things that most people find crazy, absurd…but they are real. I found a cult, followers of a creature — a demonic creature. Now I have witnessed another, followed by yet another cult."

I was horrified and intrigued at the same time. "So there is more to this than Guud's creations. Who were they?"

"The villagers…most likely all of them. I am

not sure it's a fight we want to take on. I do suggest you leave this island after we figure out the serial killer case if you're still interested."

"Yes, yes, of course, I am! But, no, Luc, I do not intend to leave, at least it's not in my plans right now, although all this is very unsettling."

He shook his head with a resigned sigh. "You are a brave woman. I will see this case to the end then, but remember, the cult is dangerous."

"How about Guud?"

"Mainland authorities seem to be staying clear of this place, and the ones that are on the island are incompetent and might even not believe us. I'm not sure about Guud yet. It seems as though he and the cult are adversaries, although they surely don't know it's his creatures who attack them."

"And the serial killer? One of them?"

"I doubt it. My gut feeling tells me it's not someone attached to a large group."

Still a mystery. "Ah. So what's next?"

"Next, I'll go down to the lighthouse, alone, and speak with Raul. When I'm back, we will draw up our next plan."

I agreed, for Luc seemed very determined not

to let me go to that region anymore.

"And what gave you inspiration about my family?"

"I met an old man, a wise man of the woods, and he gave me a clue. Sort of."

"I see," I said, but I didn't, not really.

I looked out of the window again; the kids were gone, but there was a young couple sitting on the bench now, holding each other's hands. At that moment, Alain came to mind. I wished I could have had time to get to know him better. Perhaps after all this madness was over.

"I think a lot about the world, maybe more than I should," said Luc suddenly.

He finished his second coffee and straightened his posture, ready to leave but not wanting to rush me. However, I, too, thought it was a good time.

"Where to now?" I asked him.

"We go home, and I go to the lighthouse alone."

We said farewell to the owner and headed back to the mansion.

CHAPTER TEN

Paradise Shores investigation entry number 12.
Luc Nistage.

I took another horse today. Nigel gave me a grim look of disgust as he knew that the previous horse did not come back. I just politely smiled at the old chap as I galloped away.

The air today was very cool and moist, the ocean breathing slowly and magnificently as I got closer to it, heading down the green hills towards the massive lighthouse and the little farm there belonging to a man I have not met yet, Reficul Raul.

The name itself — what kind of joke was it? Why was he all right with it? What I found oddest was others not noticing how his name, Reficul, read backwards. There was no way this was a tremendous coincidence. Would I dare to ask? The time to find out was coming as I got to the farm and tied the black horse to the fence.

A wind blew stronger, bringing that familiar essence of the ocean's secrets to my senses. I reached under my shirt right below my neck and touched the cross I have not taken off since I got it from the man who changed my life and gave me hope all those years ago. There may be some hardships up ahead as well, but helping this girl was absolutely critical. I had also decided to give up most of the money she was paying me to an orphanage upon my return to the mainland. This mission had to be about justice, but no one had to know this. I did not need to look righteous or good in the eyes of other people. True charity was secret and silent.

I walked closer to the farm. Behind a fence was a hideous short black goat. He was missing half of his right horn and seemed to have a hunch in his back. With difficulty, he stood up against the fence and stretched his head towards me. I tried to pet him, but he quickly withdrew. I understood that he was begging for food. He was indeed very thin. Was he eating well? Doubt it.

I walked along this wooden fence towards the door of the small farmhouse. Meanwhile, the sky had turned grey, and the waves began to rise and brutally punish the rocky shores and the lower walls of the giant lighthouse.

"Aaaare yu-you loookking ffffor me?"

I heard this stuttering voice behind me. As I turned around and saw this man with bad posture and messy black hair, I wondered how he had managed to sneak up on me unnoticed. This rarely happened these days.

"Raul?"

"Ccccorrect. And you?"

"Luc Nistage, private investigator. Can I ask you some questions?"

"Yes."

"You've heard of the murders in town, yes?"

"Ooof course."

"Okay. Have you seen anyone strange lately, out of place?"

"Mmmm, youu." He smiled and revealed several missing teeth.

"Hah, well yes, I am strange, an outsider, but really, anything suspicious? I've been told that you know many people on the island."

"Many people, zzzzero ffffriends."

"Ah."

I felt uncomfortable as I stood there, seemingly

hitting a dead-end in this awkward conversation. "Well, Raul. One more question. Why is your first name the way it is?"

His face instantly changed. It grew grim. His eyelids lowered, and his eyes showed clear anger. Why?

"My name is my name for a reason," he said, without stuttering this time.

I had gathered all I needed to know here. I had my theories, but now was a good time to leave without saying much more.

"Thank you for your time, Raul."

I walked away as he remained silent, staring at me angrily. I hurried to my horse, worried about what could happen. Luckily nothing did happen. When I was on my horse galloping away, I saw Raul still standing in the same spot, still facing towards the ocean. It began to rain, and I made my way back to Ida's mansion as fast as I could.

Entry 12 complete.

Now, I, Ida, will continue once again from here.

Luc sat across from me. He was watching the flames within the warm and vigorous fireplace. He told me about his strange encounter with Raul. After some time, he turned to me. "Have you had any more visions of Eleanor?"

"No, not recently. Why?"

"Just wondering. So was it her wanting to show you that you were family? Do you think she wants you to find her body?"

"To mark the grave?" I was puzzled.

"Maybe. But if you have no more visions, then...well, I guess it's over. Anyway, action must be taken soon. I'll tell you this now." Luc leaned toward me. "I went into town and saw Alain there, and I found out there have been two more victims just last night. He said he spoke with the police chief this morning. I have some ideas and suspicions but no proof. I am not certain what action to take, but I will have to do something very soon." Luc folded his hands and leaned his head on them.

An idea began to take shape in my mind. "What if I went into town at night, and you followed me in the shadows?"

"Ida, no. Use you as bait? That is very, very dangerous."

"But do you agree that it could be a way to solve this?"

Luc looked deeply into my eyes. His face was

very serious. "Yes, Ida, but let me think about it. I have another big decision to make. Two, in fact. My old self, my honorable self, just can't let it go: that Doctor Guud and that cult leader, Lief."

"I thought the cult was too dangerous to take on."

Luc flexed his hands open and closed several times. "More innocent people will suffer. If I stand by watching the evil and do nothing at all while I'm capable, then I am evil also. I will stop Guud, and at least I can hamper the cult, even if it's for a short time."

I wanted to tell him I was paying him for a different investigation, but it dawned on me that this man wasn't here for the money. He was here for redemption, destiny, and judgement. I leaned back in my chair and watched him as his eyes gleamed determinedly.

Paradise Shores investigation entry 13. Luc Nistage.

Perhaps now I have gone mad, or perhaps I am drunk with thoughts of justice and nobility, as I was when I was young.

The night was black, the stars revealing themselves

perfectly in the sky as I rode my horse towards the villages. I had found out where the man named Lief lived; there was only one man by that name on the island. His house was on the edge of the village, and that was my destination. My purpose perhaps was not one that was Christlike, but this is what I was ready to take upon my soul, and if it was wrong to stop a man like this by taking his life, then indeed I was willing to pay for it in the afterlife.

I came upon the area where I saw Theodore Blackswan's tiny home. Once again, I saw the light and, this time tied my horse near his place.

From there, I entered the dark woods again and followed my compass in the direction of the village. I kept a lookout for Guud's creatures, but my main purpose in taking this route was to avoid being seen by any other villagers. I wanted only to seek out Lief and his house. What a monster he must be, another bloodthirsty cult leader without any real humanity. Thoughts of how morally depraved this individual was gave me more confidence.

I approached each tree and bush with caution, paying attention to every sound. When I finally reached the village, I stayed on the right side and went all around the edge, still hidden by the forest. Finally, I came upon a simple long wooden home. There was light inside. As I came closer, with my revolver ready, I heard laughter. It took me aback, for it sounded like a child's laugh.

I sneaked up to one of the windows and looked in. To my shock, there on a wooden bench sat Lief, surrounded by four children. His eyes gleamed with joy, not evil, as he smiled at them and played with a wooden toy, making sounds. His children laughed. By the fire in a chair sat his wife, watching her family with happiness in her eyes. I withdrew from the window and sat down by the wall of the house. I could no longer make myself kill this man. My mind was in a scramble, with yet another twist to my experience with the nature of good and evil.

Almost fallen in spirit, I made my way back to the horse. My ride back was slow. My mind kept drawing a blank, as I found it hard to pinpoint what, exactly, I was feeling.

I wakened Ida and told her that I would not bother with the cult anymore. But tomorrow, I would confront Guud directly, in his own home. She wanted details of what had happened, but I didn't know how to explain it; therefore, I went to my room and lay in bed for hours, trying to sort my thoughts. Lief was an evil man, but to his children and wife, he was a great loving man. Would it really be correct for someone like me to decide his fate? I'd *rather leave this one for God only.*

Deep into the night, I still couldn't sleep, and I heard a movement outside my door. It sounded like someone had brushed up against it. I sat up slowly. It surely wasn't the dogs.

I pushed open the door quietly. Down the hall was a woman in a long dark dress. I could see it was dark red thanks to the moonlight, but the face was hard to make out, for a shadow fell upon it.

"Ida?"

The woman moved into the light. I felt my eyes widen. It was Eleanor, the Blackswan woman who was long dead. Her face was stern as she stared at me, then she beckoned me with a wave of her hand and faded into the wall.

I went to the window and saw her standing outside in the dark garden, watching me. I rushed to the French doors that gave out onto the garden. The air was cool and fresh. She was gone, and I frantically began to scan the gardens for her. I rounded the side of the house and saw her in the distance by the gate to the estate, and I ran there.

Eleanor was now moving towards the town, down the cobblestone path. It was brighter now due to some streetlamps. I followed swiftly. Eleanor turned into one of the streets, and I followed as she made a few more turns.

What I saw next chilled my heart, despite having had a lot of experience. The body of a dead young woman lay in the middle of a street. I wanted to kneel and examine her, but Eleanor beckoned me further. In confusion, I followed. She led me to a set of old steps leading down to a worn-out white cellar door. I walked down to it, then looked back and saw that Eleanor was gone.

I opened the door and entered an old damp cellar. It was pitch black, and I had to use a match to see. I cursed myself for not grabbing a flashlight.

It looked like nothing was there, but on the third match, I noticed a small candle in a holder on a table. I lit it and paced around the room, my senses all heightened for any aberration.

Then it happened. I felt the slightest movement of air from a spot in a wall. I began to feel and press all around it. I felt a small opening and pushed my hand in.

Part of the wall slid open, and my light showed a dank path. Something dawned on me, and I put the candle out and placed it back where I found it. Then in the dark, I stepped onto the path and closed the wall behind me. I followed the breeze in the darkness, and then I could clearly hear the waves.

I came out of a long cave-like corridor and found myself on a stony shore. I could see a rowboat, and much farther out was a larger ship, with a small light and someone standing there. I tried to focus my eyes, but then I heard a sound from the cave. I scrambled to hide behind a large rock.

A man in a mask and hood came out of the cave. Stuck in his belt was a knife. He thrust the rowboat into the water and began to row towards the ship. I stepped out of my hiding place, staying in the shadows of the rocks, and watched.

Once at the ship, the man with the knife threw a rope to the other person on deck, who helped him up, and then they pulled up the rowboat. This had to be the killer, at least one of the two. It surely wasn't Raul, but he could have been the person on the ship.

Once the ship was gone, darkness once again took over. As I stood watching the ship sail off, something began to move inside the water, and tentacles appeared. No! Not him! I screamed in horror, and as my mind went into a state of shock, I fell into the cold water.

The next thing I knew, I was waking up on a sandy beach with sunlight on my face. Someone stood over me. As my eyes got used to the bright light, I was surprised to *see that it was Lief.*

"Awake, are we?" he boomed. "Thank the sea for its mercy."

I could not have been more astonished. "Did you save me? How?"

"I was out on my boat late at night, saying my thanks to the sea...you wouldn't understand." He pointed at the cross on my neck. "Then I heard your screaming, and you were going up and under, trying to stay afloat. I rowed over and dove in. Pulled you out. The sun was coming up already...and here we are."

"Thank you...." I almost said his name but caught myself.

"My name is Lief."

"Thank you, Lief. I'm Luc." I sat up. "I must get back to town now."

"Sure you'll find your way?"

"Yes, I must hurry, but I will thank you more properly in the future."

"No need, no need. You take care."

He strode away in a slow walk, never turning around. I watched him for a moment and then rushed back into town. I knew how to catch the killer, but first, I was going to confront Guud.

As I began my walk back, I thought it strange that I could shake off the visions and dangers of the night before so quickly. And there was the fact that it had been Lief who saved me. I decided to focus on one thing at a time, in this particular moment. One thing that was certain and hampering was a crushing fatigue. When I got back to the mansion, I simply collapsed in my bed.

Entry 13 complete.

CHAPTER ELEVEN

The next morning when I went down for breakfast, I noticed Luc's door was open. He was asleep on the bed, his clothes damp and covered with sand. I was dying of curiosity, but I decided to let the exhausted man sleep. I closed the door and sat at the table, waiting for my coffee and wondering what had happened to him and where he had gone. Had he accomplished his goal with the cult?

Nigel brought my breakfast and coffee with a big smile on his face. The smell of it alone cheered me up. I knew I was neglecting my servants during this ordeal and hoped they understood. I just wanted these killings to end and to have a peaceful mind at last.

Just as I finished breakfast, Michelle hurried into the room and told me that Alain was there and wanted to see me. I rushed to the door and greeted him outside. He invited me to take a stroll, and I gladly accepted.

We leisurely walked up behind the mansion and headed down a trail with well-kept, lovely bushes and young trees surrounding us. A little way along the path was a black metal bench, which gave us a view of the town below. We sat there, enjoying unseasonal warmth.

"How's the investigation going, Ida? Are you feeling confident?"

I looked at the town, its problems hidden by the distance from which I observed, though I knew they were there. "It's been tough, but mostly because I wish I could do more. Luc has taken the investigation upon himself for the most part."

"Well, isn't that his job after all?"

"Yes, but it's important to me to contribute. The more effort, the better the result can be."

Alain gave a slight shrug. "Sometimes, it's fine to allow the expert to do the work. It worries me that you'll burn yourself out."

Touched by his concern, I smiled and replied, "I'm a bit tired now, but when it's all over, I'll be able to rest well."

"Ah…I hope it's over soon, indeed."

We spent another hour walking and ended up circling my entire property and entered the estate from the other side. I thanked Alain for coming and taking the time to help me relax and talk. He made sure I knew that the pleasure was all his, and he wished he could come more often.

After he left, I spent a long time sitting in the garden, watching the butterflies on the flowers and enjoying tea brought to me by the ever-so-kind Nigel.

Finally, Luc appeared. He had showered and changed, but still, he stumbled out of the door and sat on the chair close to mine, his eyes tired and dull. He waved to Nigel lethargically and asked for three cups of coffee.

I waited patiently while he drank the first one. Luc spoke then. "I'll go to Guud next."

"Will you tell me what happened to you? What happened with the cult? Why were you gone? And I want to go to Guud with you." I uttered the last sentence strongly and with confidence.

He looked me in the eyes, and I saw that he had no real desire to argue. His tone was resigned. "Sure. You can come, but don't be shocked at what might happen. As for the cult, it's complicated." Luc closed his eyes and massaged them with his fingers. "I don't think they'll bother you, and it's not up to us to stop them. I don't really think we can. As for the murders, I did see the killer or one of them at least."

I was surprised. "How? What? Who is it?"

"No face, but I saw where he goes, through a secret passage from the rocky part of the beach. I'll be able to get him next time."

"And how about me?"

"We can still try your plan with a great deal of caution. Ah, thank you, Nigel!"

The butler had set two more cups of coffee and a plate of waffles in front of Luc. He seemed to have forgotten his manners, for he wolfed them down, hardly stopping for breath. I supposed fatigue and exhaustion could do this to a person.

I waited until he looked like the food had done its job.

Then Luc stood up. "Are you ready to visit the good doctor?"

I nodded, and we went straight to Guud's mansion, using the same route as before.

It was getting windy, and the atmosphere grew blustery and grey. Gone was the warmth of the earlier day. The heavy clouds contributed to the sinister feeling.

Luc tried the door but with no luck. He knocked loudly, and after a long minute, Guud opened. He invited us in, and we sat in the same spot as before. He smiled at us, positioning himself in an easy chair opposite us. I wasn't sure what Luc's plan was, but it was simple, direct, and shocking.

Guud smiled a too bright, pleasant look. "What brings you here again? Did you have new questions for me? I don't have too much time."

"What did you do to those people? Why did you turn them into beasts? Monsters?"

Guud's countenance took on a look of hate. He looked startled and angry. "A 'good investigator' indeed," he hissed. "What does it matter to you? Aren't you looking for that serial killer?"

"And your actions are better?"

Guud stood up and pointed his forefinger at Luc. "I'm a scientist! People like me make the breakthroughs! You should be happy you have me!"

Luc took out his revolver and pointed it at Guud. The scientist's face grew pale as he dropped back into his chair.

"You wouldn't dare...not in front of her...."

"How many are there?"

"Five."

"How do they survive?"

"They eat. I also give them injections. It's a disease of sorts."

"So if you die, they die."

Guud gulped and stayed silent. Then his eyes got big as he realized what Luc was going to do. The shot was loud and rang in my ears. I was paralyzed with shock as I watched Guud's body roll to the floor.

We sat there for a while as Luc waited for me to recover enough to walk out. He said nothing. I stood as quickly as I could, and he hustled me out of the mansion. Then he went back in, and when he came out, I smelled smoke. By the time we had gotten a few feet into the woods surrounding the house, there was a loud explosion and fire engulfed the house. I prayed no one had seen us.

We said nothing as we took a circuitous route

back to the house. Luc helped me to my room. "Ida, you have been very brave so far. Keep being brave. This isn't over, but soon it will be. May God bless you. My sin is not your sin. Remember that. Get some rest."

He closed the door, and I was alone in the room. As I lay in bed and closed my eyes, I felt the warmth of someone near me. I knew it was Eleanor. I slowly drifted away into sleep.

I woke in the middle of the night to a thunderstorm. The branches of a tree were scratching my window, and I could hear the dogs whimpering at my door. I got up and let them in. To their surprise, I ordered them to jump up on the bed. They stopped the whimpering and stretched out on the comforter, pressing up against me. It wasn't so comfortable for me, but they made me feel safe, and perhaps that was the feeling I needed the most at the moment.

I lay awake, staring at the dark ceiling and listening to the rain. I thought a lot about loss and the afterlife. Why was Eleanor here and my grandma somewhere else? Was Eleanor trapped, or had she chosen this? This discovery of self had begun with a loss, but did I feel the souls of those gone? Right then, I felt like it was very possible to connect with them.

When the room became bright with morning sunlight, I went downstairs. No one else was up yet. I slipped on some shoes and went into the front yard. There the birds were singing with joy, greeting yet another day. Why wasn't I as happy and glad to make it through another night? To wake up alive? Those were good questions.

"Couldn't sleep more?"

I was startled by Luc's voice as I turned around and saw him standing in the doorway with a cup of black tea.

"No," I grinned, a bit embarrassed.

"Me either. Tonight is our big night. Are you ready for that?"

To my surprise, I was. "Yes."

I turned to look at the ocean view again, feeling the air. Indeed, I hoped that tonight would be the final chapter of my struggles here, an end to the terror.

Luc went back inside, and I stood there alone, listening to the nature around me. It was incredible that a person could change so much in such a short time. It was all about the intensity of events, the sheer density of it all. Luc must have been through so much more. I was grateful that he was able to help me get through this. I wished I could know more about his past, but did it really matter? I saw the man he was now, today, and it made me feel confident about our plan.

This vital day went by rather slowly and quietly. I spent most of it staying put, trying to calm my nerves. I sat outside at the little table, observing nature around me, enjoying the garden, and having meaningless but pleasant conversations with Nigel and Nella.

Finally, the night came. Luc hid his revolver and gave me a few more words of encouragement. He explained where he was going, where he wanted me to go and assured me that he would be very close, hiding in a dark alley. We waited a bit longer for the town to shut down completely and for the streets to become quiet, and for people to go home. Then it was time.

I walked through empty streets. On each side of me were shadows and dark alleys. From time to time, I could see light in a window of a house. Chills ran down my spine as I grasped the realization of what would happen to me if Luc made a mistake. I stumbled a bit and had to steady myself with a hand on a wall.

In front and above me was an old streetlight. It was periodically blinking, probably from lack of maintenance. Beyond it was a dark street. I lowered my head for a moment, examining a crack in the ground, which led all the way to the light. As I raised my head, I was momentarily paralyzed with fear as I saw a man in a mask standing there in the shadows. He had a long knife in his hand, and swiftly came towards me. I stood rooted to the spot, unable to even breathe. I closed my eyes.

Then I heard a loud shot. I opened my eyes, and the man's mask flew off his face as the bullet grazed him. It was Raul. He grimaced, as the shot wasn't fatal. Out of the alley came Luc. Raul ran into another street.

"Stay there!" Luc yelled to me as he ran after him.

I started toward him, then stopped, straining my ears as I tried to make out what was happening from the sounds. Then something caught my eye on the right side of the street. There at the corner stood another man, also in a mask. He held up a curved knife and pointed it at me.

I don't know how I gathered myself, but I began to run as fast as I could through the streets. I could hear the man chasing me. The fear caused adrenaline to course through my body, and I wasn't aware of my ragged breathing and pounding feet. I frantically ran from one street to another, searching for a lighted window or a doorway that might house someone who would help me.

Then from far off, I heard another shot. I found myself in the wide square of the wharf. There was a dark fog over the water, and I had to think fast. There was nowhere to hide, and I ran down the long pier. I rushed to the end, looking for a rowboat, but there was none. I looked back up the pier, and out of the fog came the man. I stared at him in horror.

The man removed his mask and threw it into the water. I dropped to my knees as I saw that the man was Alain. His eyes were cold and cruel as he watched me tremble.

"Raul was a good fall man. I saw him commit atrocities some time back with his fisherman friend.

Since then, I was able to satisfy my own thirst, but this time, it will be the most satisfying of all."

He raised his knife and came close to me. I tensed my body and pushed off the pier into the cold, dark sea.

Three shots boomed, muffled by the water. I surfaced and looked up at the pier.

Alain's body lay prone on the boards, blood dripping into the water below. Out of the fog came Luc, still holding his revolver. On the right side of his face was a deep cut, and there was blood all over his neck and suit.

"Ida? Ida!" he yelled in alarm.

"I'm here," I called from the water. Luc looked around for a rope and threw it down to me. I managed to climb back up onto the pier with his help.

Luc's eyes became filled with tears and sorrow as they met mine. He watched me tremble as tears rolled down my face. I could see that he understood my pain.

"I'm sorry, Ida." Then he gazed out at the foggy dark water. He said one more thing. "Such is life."

The End.

Alexander Semenyuk (also known as Oleksandr Semenyuk) is a Ukrainian-American author. He was born in Lutsk, Ukraine, in 1986. At 14, he immigrated to the United States. Alexander's favorite genres are sci-fi, horror and fantasy. Early in life, Alexander was greatly influenced by classic literature and, since childhood, dreamed of becoming a writer.

www.ingramcontent.com/pod-product-compliance
Lightning Source LLC
Chambersburg PA
CBHW020129180626
46810CB00004B/1471